Mister Fixit

Books by Elle Casey

CONTEMPORARY URBAN FANTASY

War of the Fae (10-book series)
Ten Things You Should Know About Dragons
(short story, The Dragon Chronicles)
My Vampire Summer
Aces High

DYSTOPIAN

Apocalypsis (4-book series)

SCIENCE FICTION

Drifters' Alliance (ongoing series)
Winner Takes All (short story prequel to Drifters' Alliance,
Dark Beyond the Stars Anthology)
The Ivory Tower (short story standalone, Beyond the Stars: A
Planet Too Far Anthology)

ROMANCE

By Degrees
Rebel Wheels (3-book series)
Just One Night (romantic serial)
Just One Week
Love in New York (3-book series)
Shine Not Burn (2-book series)
Bourbon Street Boys (4-book series)
Desperate Measures
Mismatched

ROMANTIC SUSPENSE

*All the Glory: How Jason Bradley Went from
Hero to Zero in Ten Seconds Flat*
Don't Make Me Beautiful
Wrecked (2-book series)

PARANORMAL

Duality (2-book series)
Monkey Business (short story)
Dreampath (short story standalone, The
Telepath Chronicles)
Pocket Full of Sunshine (short story & screenplay)

Love in New York
Book 3

Mister Fixit

ELLE CASEY

Chapter One

I DON'T WANT TO BE here in this big apartment all by myself.
Everywhere I look, I'm reminded of the love that used to dwell
here with me.

Cassie. My niece in name but every other way, my daughter…
the baby who was thrust into my life when I least expected it,
forcing me into the role of mother to a newborn at twenty-six,
much earlier than I'd planned.

But I made it work. We not only survived but thrived. She grew
new teeth. She learned to sit up. She started to eat solid food. She
can drink from a cup now and not just a bottle. I changed hun-
dreds, maybe thousands of diapers, walked the floors with her
crying in my arms, stroked her soft head when she finally did
sleep. But then her father came back from the dead and claimed
her as his, and Robinson, that bastard, made it really easy for him
to get what he wanted.

I'll never forgive him for that. Robinson could have backed out, claiming a conflict of interest or something. It wouldn't have been a lie, either. He had that conflict, or so I'd hoped. I'd been counting on the idea that after all these years of me looking at Robinson with love in my eyes that he'd finally noticed and began doing all the things he did for our family not out of obligation but out of something else — a connection to me. To my heart. I'd been so sure there was something between us. But I was wrong. I was so, so wrong.

Even if there were something there before, there isn't now. Robinson and I are over before we began, and I need to get out of here before I start breaking holes in the walls.

I grab my purse and sling it over my shoulder, taking my keys from the front-hall table as I go out the door. As I'm locking up, the door behind me opens, and my neighbor across the hall sticks her head out. That's all she's capable of doing, being that she suffers from a pretty severe case of agoraphobia.

"Jana," she whispers.

"Yes, Rose?" I turn when my lock is fully seated.

"Are you going to the grocery by any chance?"

I smile weakly. It's the best I can do when my heart's in this state. "Not right away, but I was thinking about going out later. Why? Do you need something I can grab for you?" I know for a fact she has her groceries delivered, but once in a while when she only needs something small, she'll ask me to buy it for her. I don't mind. She seems like a nice woman, even though I don't know her very well.

"Oh, that's okay, I don't want to bother you." She starts pulling her head back inside.

"No, it's fine, Rose." I make an effort at using a cheerier tone. "I'm sorry if I sound so blasé right now. I'm just … tired."

Rose's head re-emerges. For some reason seeing her head coming out like that reminds me of a baby being born, and I lose my smile.

"What's the matter?" She smiles kindly. "Baby keeping you up at night again?" She never complained about Casssie's crying, even though I knew she could hear it on the few occasions I would stay here in the city and not out in Brooklyn. My other neighbors weren't nearly as understanding, which is why I spent more time out at Jeremy's place than I did here.

"No." I try to say more, but I can't. My mouth starts to tremble and tears rush to fill my eyes.

Rose's face falls. "Oh, dear. Have I said something wrong? Would you like to come in for some tea?"

I've never been inside Rose's apartment, always leaving her requested grocery items with her at the door, but the need to be with another human being and curiosity have me saying yes to her offer. I need a distraction from all this emotion and maybe she can be that for me right now.

"Come in, come in," she says, waving at me from a door open wider than I've ever seen from her.

I walk in with my eyes bugging out. I had assumed that along with agoraphobia, Rose would also suffer from pathological hoarding. I don't know why; my own ignorance, I suppose. But as soon as I'm just two steps into the place, I realize she's anything but.

After entering her foyer, I follow her into another room, past antiques I know to be worth a fortune. We enter a formal living room that's at least three times the size of mine.

I smile as a few mysteries connect and finally make sense. No wonder those doors next to hers never opened. She owns the space behind all of them, having combined three apartments into one giant place. I thought my apartment was a good investment, but hers puts mine to shame.

"Is Earl Grey okay with you, or do you prefer herbal tea?" She shuffles off to the kitchen.

I watch her go, admiring her dark blue kaftan paired with black pants. Even though she never leaves the apartment, she's dressed as if she's about to go shopping and have lunch with a wealthy friend. Her hair and makeup are flawless, which is saying a lot for a woman of her age, and I estimate that to be about eighty-five. Both of my grandmothers eschewed makeup in their later years, claiming it was more trouble than it was worth.

"I'll have whatever you're having." I raise my voice to be heard in the other room. "I don't want to be any trouble."

"Oh, it's no trouble, believe me. I'm glad of the company. Tea is always better when shared." She reappears at the entry to the room. "Have a seat, dear. I'll be back in a jiffy." She points to a chair and turns around, tottering a little and holding the wall for a moment for support.

I never noticed any hints of frailty in her before, but then I guess that's not surprising since I only ever see her head. Who knows, she could be falling all over the place in here, and I'd never find out about it until an ambulance showed up. Jesus, I'm a shit neighbor.

Imagining her lying on this carpet here with no way to communicate amplifies my concern for her wellbeing. Should she even be living here on her own? I should probably pry a little when she gets here with the tea. Maybe she has a son or a daughter who checks in on her that I've never noticed. That would be nice; then I won't have to worry quite as much.

Before taking the seat she suggested, I wander over to some shelves on the far wall. There are no photographs to identify any children in her life, just books and archeological artifacts that look like ancient deities carved out of stone, very worn in some places. I'm tempted to touch one of them, but I resist. I've been to enough museums with *Do Not Touch* signs on them that my instincts tell me to keep my hands to myself.

Her books range from the classics to references on the Bronze Age, Polytheism, and the Middle East. I'm just about to reach for one of them when a noise behind me distracts me and makes me turn around.

A cat is sitting on the nearby table, staring at me.

I rest my hand on my chest, my heart fluttering underneath at an abnormally fast rate. "Kitty, you scared me." I walk over with my hand held out. The cat merely watches me. "I didn't know you lived here." I attempt to stroke her head, but she moves away, absolutely not interested in any attention from me. I'll be honest; the rejection stings.

I frown at her. What kind of cat doesn't want a little stroke now and then? She walks along the back of a couch, and I follow with my hand out. "Come here, Kitty, I just want to pet you." My crazy brain is thinking she's just misunderstood my motives. As soon as she realizes I'm only there to be her servant, she'll jump right up for the opportunity.

She leaps from the couch to a chair, and I'm right behind her. "Just one pet. Come on, you know you like it." It's become a personal challenge. She thinks she doesn't want attention from me, but she's wrong. As soon as she gets one little tickle behind the ear, she'll want more. I'm great with cats.

I nearly pounce on her as I reach the chair, but she's too fast for me. She leaps to the floor and skitters across the wood parquet, escaping through the legs of her owner into the room beyond.

Rose looks down at the cat and then up at me, bewildered. "Well! I guess she's in a hurry to get somewhere."

My face grows pink as I wonder whether Rose saw me chasing her cat around the room. How embarrassing. When have I ever been invited into someone's home and then proceeded to terrorize their family pet? What's gotten into me? Why am I acting so strangely? So the cat didn't want any affection from me. Is that a crime now? And why do I feel so utterly rejected? It's just a damn cat, and not a very friendly one at that.

"Here, let me help you," I say, moving across the room to take the tea tray from her. It looks heavy, and I need the distraction.

"Oh, that's okay, I have everything in hand. If you'll just move those magazines out of the way for me." I follow her gaze to the coffee table that has four magazines spread out around it. One is a *Vogue*, the others are all journals of some sort.

Turning to move them out of her path, I smile, still feeling awkward over harassing her poor cat. "What a beautiful tea service that is," I say, hoping she'll forget about how fast her kitty was moving when he left. "I rarely see the real thing anymore."

"Yes, well, I tend to be a little old-fashioned, you could say."

I try to keep smiling, but now I'm feeling even worse. First I stalk her cat, then I tell her she's a fuddy duddy. "No, I didn't

mean it that way. I really do like it. Some things shouldn't change."
I stand and give her my best smile, willing my lips not to tremble.

She laughs as she puts the tray down, the cups and saucers clinking together as they rattle around. "Oh, not to worry, dear. I didn't take offense."

I sit down in a nearby wing-backed chair and fold my hands in my lap. I'm probably better off treating this whole place like a museum at this point. I seem to have lost both my grace and my manners, and Rose seems like the kind of person who's used to having those things around.

She starts to pour some tea into one of the cups. "So, you chased Mumfry right out of the room, eh?"

I nearly choke on my own saliva.

Chapter Two

SHE CHUCKLES. "HE'S THE MOST pig-headed pussycat that ever lived. Don't take it personally if he didn't let you pet him." She holds up the saucer and cup. "Sugar, dear?"

My face if flaming red and I've started to perspire. I feel like I'm being punked by an eighty-five year old recluse. Not my proudest moment. "Yes, one please. Thank you. No milk."

She fixes my tea and then stirs, speaking absently as the liquid swirls around inside the cup. "He lets me pet him once a week. Twice if it's Christmas."

My laughter sounds fake, even though it's not. "Why twice at Christmas?"

She takes her own teacup and drops a lump of sugar into it. "Because I feed him foie gras on Christmas Eve. It's the one day of the year he gets something special, and he rewards me with access to his head for about five seconds." She looks off into the distance. "He reminds me of my late husband, actually."

When I laugh this time, it sounds more genuine. "Not very af-fectionate, I take it?" I take my tea and saucer in hand. Sipping,

I watch her over the rim. She's way more feisty than I originally thought she would be.

"No, not really. A scientist. Archeologist, actually." She sighs and puts her cup down. "He was always more interested in artifacts than any living thing."

I twist around toward her shelves. "I noticed you have some artifacts there."

"Yes, I've winnowed down our original collection, leaving just my favorites here. The rest are on loan."

"Really? Where?" Our family has some pieces on loan too, although I don't really know what they are specifically, other than the fact that they're paintings. My brother James always kept track of those things for us. And now that our parents are gone, none of us is really interested in getting the stuff back. Better to let the public enjoy them than locking them away where only we can see them. Thanks to our grandparents' and parents' investments, none of us will ever have to sell one of the pieces for money to live on.

She waves her hand carelessly. "Oh, we have things here in Manhattan. London. Dubai if you can believe that." She rolls her eyes.

"Dubai? That's really cool, actually."

She shrugs. "Ancient artifacts have been in my life for over sixty years. I'm kind of tired of the whole game, really. I have other interests now."

I turn back to her, more curious than ever. "Like what?" I don't know what I expect her to say, maybe lion-taming or something equally daring since her career path makes me think of Indiana Jones, but I'm surprised nonetheless when she gives me her actual answer.

"Knitting if you can believe it." She laughs as if she can't believe it herself. "Of all the things." She shakes her head. "It's just that my mind starts racing, and since I don't go out anymore, there's nothing to rein it in. The knitting is very calming. Very relaxing."

"Maybe I should try it." The words fly out of my mouth out of sense of politeness, but I should have watched what I was saying more closely. I've revealed too much, and I'm quickly learning that just because Rose stays inside all the time, it doesn't mean she isn't as sharp as a tack.

She sips her tea and smiles. "So tell me, Jana. Where's little Cassie today?"

I swallow and make a big show of picking up my tea and sipping, giving me time to compose myself before I respond.

"I can't remember the last time I heard her, actually." Rose tips her head, waiting for my answer.

"Well, uh, it's because… Cassie's with her father." Why was that so hard to say? Probably because I wanted to say, 'Cassie's with her drug addict no-show dad who I had to pick up the pieces for.' But it wouldn't have been very neighborly to share that much dirty laundry, so instead I stutter my way through the polite answer.

She frowns. "I seem to recall you telling me her father wasn't able to care for her."

Whoops. Guess I shared a little bit of that laundry already. Oh well. "He wasn't. But he is now. Apparently." I nearly choke on that last word. I have to quickly put the teacup in my face again to keep from crying.

"He's your brother, right?"

Rose also has a great memory. Faaaantastic. "Yes. My brother Jeremy. He lost his wife almost a year ago. In March it'll be a year." Guilt assails me. Here I am giving him shit in my head about dumping Cassie on me, when I know very well why he did it. He had his reasons and no one blamed him for them; no one except me, of course, but only after he took Cassie back.

"That's right," Rose says. "I read about it in the papers, and I remember her funeral." She gives me a sad smile. "I'm sorry I couldn't go."

I shake my head, not wanting her to go down that road. "No, it's fine. Really. I didn't expect you to." I put my teacup down, my drink finished, anxious to leave. I thought having some company would be good for me, but I was wrong. I feel like shit and pretending to be a happy person is taking more energy than I have.

"So your brother has Cassie now? And he's okay?"

I hang onto the arms of the chair to help steady my emotions. "Yes. He and his girlfriend. Or his wife, I guess she is now." It's impossible to miss the bitterness in my voice. I blame everything on her, which may or may not be fair, but that's how I'm playing it. Before she came along, everything was fine. Well, okay, it wasn't fine; Jeremy was going to hell in a hand basket, but Cassie was great, and I was great. Why did anything have to change? Jeremy could have gotten better and left Cassie with me. I was already acting as her mother…

"That must be hard for you," Rose says, oblivious to my internal struggle, "raising her for all those months and then having her taken away." She puts her teacup down. "You still see her, though, I imagine." She waits for me to reassure her.

"Yes, of course. I'm welcome at their home anytime I want to be there."

"Do you go? Do you visit?"

I shrug. "I want to."

"But you don't." She lowers her chin, but keeps her eyes on me. She looks like a grade school teacher waiting for me to admit I didn't do my homework.

I shake my head, my heart aching. "No. I think about it a lot, but I just don't think it's a good idea."

"Why not?"

"Because… she's settling into her new life, with her dad and her … new mother." My voice catches on the last word. I hate that girl who took my place in Cassie's life. *Sarah*. The mere word alone makes me want to spit on this pretty Aubusson carpet.

Rose's face goes soft. "Aww, honey, she's not taking your place."

I frown, wondering if Rose is reading my mind at this point.

She continues. "You're going to be the most special aunt that little girl will ever have. No one can take that away from you."

I wave my hand around, trying to dissipate the heavy emotions that are hanging over our teatime. "No, I know that. I'm not worried about it. I saw them at my brother's wedding, and everything was fine. I'm just busy. Actually, I'm thinking about buying a fixer-upper and doing the work myself."

She sits back, a smile lighting up her face. "Really? Well, that's exciting. And that'll keep you busy, that's for sure. Not something you could have done with a baby around." She puts her hands on her thighs. "Good for you. When will you start?"

I had only been tossing the idea around in my head before, but now that I've said it out loud, it seems like the perfect plan. I have money, I have time, and I have way too much going on in my head. Like Rose said, I need a distraction.

"Today. I was just heading out to go house hunting." I'm immediately energized, like everything I've been doing for the past month has been a complete waste of time. Mooning around my apartment, mourning the loss of my pseudo-motherhood … it was a mistake. Life is what it is, and I can't change most of it. Why cry over the parts I have no control over? There's no point. I can change this part, the part where I have too much time on my hands, and I can do it now. The only thing stopping me is not having a property.

"Do you have a realtor?" she asks.

I shake my head, realizing as she posed the question that I haven't done a single thing yet to prepare myself for this grand adventure. My parents, were they still alive, would listen to me now and tell me I was completely nuts and suggest I seek therapy. Rose, on the other hand, stands and walks over to a gorgeous walnut desk in the corner of the room near her shelves. "I have a friend whose son is a realtor. He specializes in this kind of thing if you'd like his number."

"Sure. Of course. That'd be great."

She takes out a binder filled with business cards and then carefully transcribes a number from one of them to a piece of paper. After putting everything back in its place, she walks over to me and hands her note over. "His name is Dicky. His father and my husband were colleagues."

I look at the careful script on the page. "Dicky Dickerson," I say, trying to keep a straight face.

Rose sighs. "Yes, not very nice of his parents, was it?"

I burst out laughing and then throw my hand up over my mouth to try and stop more hilarity from coming out. I'm liable to get rolling and be unable to stop if I'm not careful. My emotions are teetering on the edge of crazytown.

Rose pats me on the shoulder and goes back to her chair. "Some people just can't see any farther than the ends of their noses, can they? Lucky for us, we're more self-aware than that."

I bite my lip to keep from laughing again.

"Would you like some more tea?" She leans forward in anticipation of a yes.

I stand. "No, thank you. I need to get going." I hold the paper out and wave it a little. "I have to give Mr. Dickerson a call and see what I can find out there. I'm anxious to get started."

She stands, using her hands on her thighs to steady herself. "Thank you for stopping by. You're welcome any time, you know." We walk to the front door together. "I hope you don't plan to move into that fixer upper after you're done with it."

"I don't know what I'll do, but I like my apartment." I don't say it aloud, but I like it even more now that I know Rose a little better. I had no idea she was so interesting.

"Good. It's hard to find good neighbors these days." She sighs, and I know she's got to be thinking about the couple down the hall. I've never seen anyone party as hearty as they do.

"Don't I know it." I lean in to kiss her on the cheek. "Take care." I'm about to walk out and then stop when I remember something. "What was it that you wanted from the grocery store?"

"Oh, yes! I forgot. I need some butter."

"Do you want some now? I have a stick or two in my fridge."

"No, no, that's all right. It's not urgent. And if you don't make it to the store, don't worry. I can wait for my toast until tomorrow when my regular delivery comes."

I wiggle my fingers in a wave as I leave, and while I walk down the hall, I punch out the phone number of Mr. Dicky Dickerson on my cell. Maybe having a realtor helping me out wouldn't be such a bad idea.

Chapter Three

DICKY DICKERSON WAS TOO BUSY to meet with me today, but that's not going to stop me. I'm cruising through some of my favorite neighborhoods in Brooklyn, searching for signs. Specifically, *For Sale* signs, but I'd even take a cosmic sign at this point. This feels right. I'm doing what I should be doing, I can sense it in my bones.

My cell rings, but I don't recognize the number. Thinking it might be Dicky, I use my professional voice. "Hello, this is Jana Oliver."

The person who responds is goofing around, pretending to be formal. "Well, hello, Ms. Jana Oliver. And how might you be this afternoon?" When he laughs, I realize who it is, and my emotions instantly go cold.

"I'm fine. What do you want, Robinson?" I sigh out heavily, hoping he'll take the hint that I'm not in the mood to chat.

"Whoa. Cold reception. Okay. I'm going to assume it's not because of something I've done, though, and…"

I cut him off. "Oh yeah? And why would you do that, I wonder?"

There's no response for long enough that I start to think we got cut off. But then there's a long sigh and his voice has lost all its cheerfulness. "So you are blaming me for everything."

If I could throw my phone out the window and not regret its loss, I totally would right now. As it is, I'm about to crack it in half with how hard I'm gripping it.

"Now why would I do that?" I say, pretending to be super duper happy as I sit at a stoplight. "You're not the guy who made me the legal parent of my niece, encouraged me to bond with her as her mother, and then as soon as my brother stopped doing drugs for a single day, undid all the legal ties between her and me and forced me to give her up!" I pause. "Oh, wait…! I'm wrong! That *was* you, Robinson!" I'm screaming now, but I don't care. People in the neighboring cars can stare all they want.

He sounds like a lawyer when he speaks this time. "You know very well that's not how things went down."

"Oh really?" A car honks behind me, telling me to obey the green light. I flip him off out my rear window before I press on the gas. "Really? Because that's exactly how I remember it. You did that, Robinson. *You* took her away from me."

"You know, I saw you at the wedding, and you seemed fine with everything."

"And because you know me sooo well, you're the best person to judge whether I'm okay, right? Is that it?"

"Listen, Jana, do you want to talk? In person, I mean, not on the phone? You sound really angry."

All I can do is scream at that. I reach out and try to press the red button on my phone to close down the call, but it won't work. I can still hear Robinson's voice, but none of the words are computing. I just need to never listen to him again. Ever. I yank the power cord out of the bottom of the phone, roll down the window, and toss the cell out into the street where it bounces up and skitters onto the nearby sidewalk. I catch the shocked look of a girl as my phone lands at her feet.

I'm so pissed, I feel like I can't even trust myself not to drive my car into a wall. I continue down the road, using the steering wheel to shake my body forward and back, over and over, screaming in frustration the whole time.

Great! Excellent! Now I have no phone *and* no baby! It's all Robinson's fault, too. Who's that stupid? Who's that clueless about life? I reach the next red light and slump back into my seat. Robinson, that's who. He's that clueless.

Of course I'm furious with him. No woman on the face of the earth would take in a child, love her like her own, and then just hand her over with a smile and a 'Good luck, I hope things work out for ya.' I was devastated, I *am* devastated, and I will *always* be devastated. And if it hadn't been for *him*, that snake in a lawyer's suit, I'd still be driving around with a babyseat in my car and diapers stinking up my guestroom.

The light changes to green and I pull away, but within two blocks I'm crying so hard I have to pull over onto a side street. It's not until someone taps on my window that I realize I'm on the side of the road in a not-so-great area, and there's a For Sale sign in the yard right next to me. I could throw my phone out the window and hit it easily, if I had a phone anymore.

"You okay, Miss?" the man at my window asks me. He could be homeless, the way he's dressed, or he could just be one of those wannabe beatnik cool guys who hangs around the streets of Brooklyn.

I nod, wiping tear streaks from my face with the heels of my hands. "Yes, I'm fine," I answer through the closed window. My hand moves to the ignition, but just before I turn the key, I realize my engine is already on. I've been sitting here for I don't know how long idling, spewing carbon monoxide out into the atmosphere. I'm sure the people living on this street really appreciate that.

"You sure? You look sad to me." He frowns and points to his cheeks.

"No, really, I'm fine." I glance over at the house that's for sale and then at him. "Do you live around here?"

"You could say that." He smiles, revealing teeth in sore need of dentistry.

"Do you know what the story is with this place?" I jab my thumb over at the sign.

He looks over my car at it, frowns, and then drops his gaze to me again. "Been for sale for a long time. Nobody livin' in it. That's all I know."

I grab a pen from my purse and a little notebook, writing down the name of the realtor I see on the sign and her phone number along with the street number for the house. I'll get the street name when I drive out of here.

Idiot me threw my phone out the window, so now I have to wait until I'm home again to call anyone. And that Dicky character will probably call me while my phone's with that lucky stranger who I nearly nailed with it, so I guess I won't be meeting anyone today to hunt for houses. I want to bang my head on my steering wheel in frustration. Can nothing go right for me?

"You got any spare change?" the man asks, distracting me from my thoughts.

"Sure," I say distractedly, reaching into my wallet for some bills. "Here you go." I slide them through a three-inch space I make rolling the window down. It's too cold to let all the heat out.

"Ten bucks, hey, thanks." He gives me a genuine smile, which only makes me feel guilty. My heart lurches over the idea of ten bucks making my day. "Here," I say, giving him the rest of what I have. "Take it."

He frowns as the wad of bills come through the crack. "You sure you're okay?"

I nod, facing out the front of the window. "I will be."

He takes the money and backs away from the car. "You have a nice day, Miss."

"You too," I say, shifting the car into gear and pulling away from the curb. Time to go get a new phone and find a house to buy. I'm going to do this. This is going to happen. I can't stay in my apartment anymore; it's too depressing and I'm going crazy staring at its four walls. Rose is awesome, and I'll visit her, but I can't live there right now. Not with all those memories tied to it. Plus, I need a job to do, one that has me as the boss. I'm in no emotional state to be working retail again. Besides, how hard can being a general contractor be, anyway? My late sister-in-law did it, and she made it look really easy. I'm college-educated, smart, and talented in the design department. And it's been said before: once I put my mind to something, I can make it happen. I glance at the rundown house with the sagging porch outside as I drive past it and smile. Watch out, World, here I come.

Chapter Four

THERE ARE THREE VOICEMAILS FROM Robinson, one from James, and eight from Leah on my new phone when I get it up and running the next day. I listen to Robinson's on speakerphone as I get dressed in house hunting clothes. Today will be the day that I find a place to renovate. After a fitful night's sleep and way too much time imagining all the things I could get accomplished, there's no way it's not going to work. I've got it all figured out.

As soon as I hear the initial part of Robinson's first message, I stride across the room to the counter where my new phone rests. "Hey, Jana, it's me. Robinson. Listen, I really think you've got this all wrong…"

Click. Delete. "Goodbye, Robinson, you jerk." I smile in the mirror, but it doesn't look happy. The next message comes on.

"Are you ignoring me?"

Click. Delete. "Gee, you think? Asshole." I shake my head. He can't possibly be that stupid.

I wait for the next message. There's some fumbling around and then his voice again. "If you're ignoring me, tell me. Otherwise, I'm coming over. I'm worried about you."

My eyes bug out as I hear the time the message was sent. I look at my watch. An hour ago. Holy shit, I have to get out of here. I don't want to see him; I'm likely to punch him right in the nose.

The doorbell rings a half-second later. Not my intercom buzzer, but my actual door. How in the hell did he get inside? Stupid neighbors. Someone in this building needs a bitch-slap.

"Goddammit!" I hiss. I jerk a brush through my hair, wincing as I accidentally yank some strands out in my anger. "Go away, jerk, I don't want you here," I say mostly to myself. I plan to ignore his knocking. He'll go away eventually.

I check my watch again as the doorbell rings. I'm supposed to meet this Dicky person at the home that I saw for sale yesterday in a half hour. Word on the realtor street is that it's about to go into foreclosure and the owners are ready to deal. I just need Robinson to go away so I can get there on time.

The doorbell rings a third time. "I know you're home!" comes a voice through the door. "I saw your car downstairs!"

I sneer at my reflection in the mirror. He'd better not force the issue. I destroyed a phone yesterday, I was so mad; there's no telling what I'm capable of doing if I see him in person.

"Come on, Jana, talk to me!"

He's going to make me late. I need to do something about this. I slam the brush down on the counter and stare at myself in the mirror. "You can do this. Cut him off. Make him go away. It's over. You're never going to be with him, so just forget it."

Okay, I'll admit it. I've had a crush on Robinson since the first time I met him. Actually, since the first time I laid eyes on him, when I saw him in a photo with my brother. This is even more pitiful when you consider how old I was at the time: six. Yes. I was *six* years old when I fell in love with Robinson Arnold.

It was Christmas break, my brother's first semester of college, and he came home with mementoes of his new life. Robinson was his roommate and new best friend. I still remember the way that picture of him made my blood race in my veins, and I was just a little kid. A baby, practically. But something about this boy made me feel funny inside. He was my first crush.

And when I finally met him in person after the next semester, it was ten times worse. I thought I was having a heart attack when he smiled at me. I was only a little girl, but there was something about this boy that was different from every other one I'd ever met. When I played with my Barbies, he was my Ken, when I playacted being Cinderella, he was my Prince Charming, and as I grew older, he became the man that every other guy was measured against.

Over the years, I've gotten better at hiding my reactions — my brothers used to tease me that my face would light up like Times Square whenever his name was mentioned — but my feelings stayed strong, even more than two decades and several boyfriends later. But now it's over. I'm done with loving him, with crushing on him, with dreaming about being with him. Not like it's a big deal to anyone but me that this ridiculous wannabe love affair is over; he never saw me as anything but James's little sister.

I'm on the other side of the door when he bangs on it with his fist. "Jana, so help me, if you don't open this door, I'm going to…"

I flip the lock and throw the door open. "You're going to what? Take my child away from me? Oh, wait. That's right. You already did that." I stand there with my arms folded across my chest, waiting for him to walk away.

His shoulders sag. "Come on, Jana, you don't really believe that."

"Go away, Robinson. I'm done talking to you."

He takes a step forward. "Can't I just come in for a minute?"

I reach an arm out and push on his chest. "No. Not even for a second." I start to close the door, but he puts his hand on it and stops me.

"Wait!"

I stand there, glaring at him, fighting the tears that will give my hurt feelings away. I want him to think I'm just mad, seething with pure anger. I don't want him to see how deeply he hurt me by standing against me in this thing with Cassie.

"I have to go," I say through closed teeth.

"You can take one minute to listen to what I have to say."

"I could, but I won't." I try to shut the door, but he's stronger than me.

"Come on, Jana, stop being so bull-headed about this, would you?"

The door across the hall cracks open just the slightest bit. That's when I realize that I'm putting on a show for the neighbors. Grabbing him by the front of the shirt, I yank him toward me and pull him into the apartment.

"That was a quick change of heart," he says, talking past a new smile.

I shut the door and respond in an angry whisper. "Don't get excited, I was just keeping my problems from becoming the next building soap opera. Thanks for banging on my door and alerting everyone who lives on the block that I have issues."

"Sorry," he says, shrugging, "but I called several times. I rang the bell. You can't avoid me forever, you know."

I raise my eyebrows at him and laugh. "Oh yeah? Says who?"

"Says me." He seems just as shocked at I am. "We're family."

I shake my head. "I have news for you, Robinson. You're wrong; we're *not* family. You're my brother's friend and the family attorney. But after that stunt you pulled, you can consider yourself fired from that job. You don't represent my interests anymore. I'm done." I open the door and gesture with my free hand. "Please leave."

"You don't mean that."

His serious expression makes him look very old. Why did I never notice that about him before? Why had his youth and good looks remained frozen in time for me? Now I can see him for what he really is: old, mean, heartless, and stupid. I can do so much better. I've wasted enough of my life on this turd.

"I meant every word. Now get out, or I'm calling the police."

He steps over the threshold and turns halfway to deliver his parting shot.

"I'm not going to give up that easily."

I laugh as I slam the door in his face, yelling so he'll hear me through the thick wood. "Give up! It's over!"

The sound of footsteps going down the hall leaves me breathing easier. Good. That's done. Now I'm free to live my life how I want to live it, without some jerk telling me what's best for me and the people I love.

Taking my purse and keys from the table, I leave the apartment for my appointment with Dicky, my heart much heavier than I want it to be. Today is the first day of the rest of my life, and I've already jettisoned some dead weight. Things are looking up. I just need to keep telling myself that until it really feels that way.

Chapter Five

IT'S AMAZING HOW FAST CASH talks in Manhattan. Three weeks after seeing the house for the first time, Dicky hands me the keys to the front door. "Congratulations. You are now the proud owner of a bona fide fixer upper." His grin slips, and I know why. He advised me against taking on such a big project for my first attempt. I ignored him, of course, because he doesn't know me or the power of my determination.

"Thank you, Dicky. For everything. You work fast."

He shrugs. "Money talks, BS walks. You got them out of a financial bind, and they should be grateful."

"I doubt very highly that 'grateful' is the word they're using right now." Dicky bargained them down about twenty percent from what they were asking, but it's not like we dragged them over any hot coals to get there. When I did my first walk-through and saw the insults spray-painted on the walls, the holes in the plaster, and the torn up floors, I knew they were dreaming with the price tag they'd put on it. Divorces are not pretty, but divorces that include property in Manhattan? Downright ugly sometimes.

"Their loss, your gain, right? And I have no doubt that you'll turn that place around."

We walk out of the title agent's office together and down the elevator into the parking garage. "You sure you're not worried?" I tease. "You looked a little doubtful there when I said I was going to be the GC."

He shrugs. "What do I know? Maybe you'll be a natural. But remember," he waits for me to exit the elevator ahead of him, "there's no shame in admitting you're in over your head and calling in a professional."

His lack of confidence stings, but I don't let it show. "Thanks for the advice. See you around?"

He shakes my hand where we've stopped at the back of my car. "With pleasure. You know where to find me if you need me." He walks off and shouts over his shoulder. "When you're ready for your next project, give me a call!"

"Sure thing!" I get into my car and sit there for a few minutes staring out the front windshield. I am officially the proud owner of a new home with a tiny front and back yard in an area of Brooklyn that's not too far from some of my favorite places. I smile in satisfaction. Now it's time to get to work.

I've been looking forward to this distraction for three weeks now. Having to put Leah, James, and Jeremy off every time they've called has been difficult, but now I have a real excuse. I try a few new ones in my head for practice:

Sorry, can't come to family dinner because I have some drywall to repair.

Sorry, can't come shopping with you because I have new flooring going in.

Sorry, no, I don't have time for visitors today; I have to go buy ten gallons of paint.

The release from the pressure of all the lies I've had to make up will be very welcome. I can only have so many hair appointments, friends with birthdays, and contagious chest colds before people start getting pushy with me. As it is, they were pretty much at that point. Just today, Jeremy left me a voicemail telling me they expected me on Sunday for family spaghetti night, and they weren't going to take no for an answer.

"Sorry," I say out into the car's interior as I reverse out of my parking space, "I'm busy moving into my new place. I'll catch you next month, maybe. And oh, by the way, if Robinson's going to be there, I won't be." I know it'll cause a stink to throw in that little caveat, but that's too bad. If they want me there, they're going to have to choose: me or him. And if they choose him, fine. It might be easier that way. I have a lot of work to get done on my new house. I could dwell on how painful it is for me to see Cassie now, but I won't go there. Those are floodgates I just can't open right now.

My first stop after signing for the title to the house is the home improvement store. I spend an hour in there, interrogating a poor salesman about how to do drywall repair. I also purchase a set of work overalls, shoe covers, a gas mask, and a painter's hat. I don't want to get my clothes dirty, do I? Also in my cart go the materials recommended for my drywall repair, a new door lock, and some tools. Several men in the aisles were happy to give me advice about what I'd need. One even pointed out a shiny, red toolbox he said he wished he could buy for himself. He put it in my cart for me since it was kind of heavy.

My car sinks down in the back with the weight of everything I bought. I frown at it and look over at the other vehicles in the lot. It makes me wonder if a GC should be driving a truck and not a Volvo. I'll have to think on that while I'm covering up all the holes in my walls and installing a new front door lock with my brand new tools. I'm so excited, I practically skip over to the driver's side door and get in. So far, this general contractor stuff has turned out to be a cakewalk. At least I know I'm good at the shopping part.

My second stop after getting my keys and construction materials is the grocery store. I can't very well get started on a long workday without something to eat or drink, now can I? I stock up on the basics and grab a cheap coffee maker while I'm at it. I have one back at my apartment, but I plan to rent the place out furnished, so I need to leave almost everything there. I'll get the rest of what I need later.

Two hours after signing the papers, I pull into the space in front of the house and smile at my new home. It's all mine, bought and paid for with cash. I can already see what the exterior will look like; I'll bring out all the Craftsman details and get rid of the changes that were made to it by people who didn't know what they were doing. I'll start by demolishing that sagging porch and putting it back to the way it should be. I've got several photos on my *Pinterest* boards with inspiration for the whole project.

The first thing I notice when I enter is a terrible odor. My nose crinkles in response. Why didn't I smell that before? Is it new? I haven't been here since my inspection walk-through two weeks ago. The stench is a cross between old cheese and rotten garbage. I tiptoe over some random trash strewn across the living room floor and enter the kitchen. There, in the middle of the linoleum, is a dead rat.

"Oh my god!"

I scream, running back to the front door and out onto the front porch. Standing on what might someday be a lawn, huffing and puffing, I wonder what I should do next and how I got in this situation in the first place. Why is there a rat there? Did the former owners come in and put it there, or is my new kitchen the place where vermin come to die? The thought makes me shudder.

Five minutes later, I'm freezing my ass off and no closer to a solution. The only thing I do finally figure out is that I can't let this stop me. The sub-zero temperature may be contributing to this thought process, but I'm going to go with it. I'm the GC, so what would a real GC do in a situation like this? He'd call someone, that's what. I pull my phone from my purse and call my cleaning lady.

"Estelle? Hi, this is Jana."

She says a bunch of things in Spanish, and when she stops, I speak again. "Are you free? Because I bought that house I told you about, and there's a dead rat in here on the floor, and I need someone to come clean this place up."

The tone of her voice goes decidedly rude and then she hangs up.

I've told her a thousand times I don't speak Spanish, but does she listen? No. But for the past six months, that hasn't interfered in our ability to communicate. At least not until now. Maybe I shouldn't have told her about the rat until she got here.

I chew my lip, wondering what to do next. Since I don't have wifi yet and my computer's at my apartment, I have no way of looking up a business that deals with this sort of thing. What would I use as my search terms? Rats-B-Gone? It wouldn't be an exterminator because the rat already exterminated itself. Is there such a thing as rat removal services? I'll probably never know, because the longer I wait out here, the longer it'll be before I'm fixing all those holes in the wall, and I promised myself I'm going to move into this place by the weekend. That gives me five days to get things done.

Just the idea of smooth walls gets me pumped up again. I walk into the front hall with a confident stride and my gaze falls on my shopping bags. A smile lights up my face as the solution comes to me — the solution that's been staring at me this whole time. I tear into several packages and relieve them of their offerings.

Now dressed in my worker overalls, thick rubber gloves, a painting gas mask with canisters attached, a painter's hat covering every strand of my hair, and rubber workboots that go up to my knees, I am properly attired. *Bring it, you nasty dead rat.* The disgusting broom that I found in the pantry, its bristles permanently folded to the side and covered in old dirt, will be perfect for what I need to do.

In the kitchen again, I prod the rat a couple times to be sure he's really dead and not just taking a ratnap on my kitchen floor. His entire body moves with the stiffness of a corpse, so I'm no longer worried about him waking up and making a mad dash for my leg.

I use the small kitchen broom like a big industrial push broom, moving him across the floors and out to the front hall. As I pass other garbage, I add it to my pile. Pretty soon I have what looks like an entire bag's worth in front of me.

Seeing the somewhat clean streak behind me inspires me to do more. Soon, I have half the trash from the living room pushed into the front hall, and it's knee deep against the wall. I'm actually making progress. At this point, I'll be able to move in by Friday!

Taking a moment to relish the fruits of my labors, I lean on my broom in the middle of the living room, nodding. So far so good. I don't know why everyone kept giving me that funny look when I said I was going to be the GC.

It's just at that moment when I'm patting myself on the back that Fate decides to remind me that I should always find some wood to knock on when I speak out loud about being in control of my life.

Something, I have no idea what, lands on the top of my head, hits my shoulder, and then falls to the floor next to my leg.

My first thought arrives with a flash of fear: *Is the ceiling falling down around my ears now? That can't be good.*

When I look down and see a mouse, stunned, but still very much alive lying on its side just next to my foot, I have a second thought: *Is it raining mice in my house?* In stunned horror, I lift my eyes to the ceiling, trying to figure out how a mouse managed to land on my *head.*

There, where there should be a light fixture, is a hole in the ceiling and another tiny mouse face looking down at me. His whiskers twitch and then he leans out farther, his entire upper body straining downward. At my face.

I run screaming from the living room, tripping over the giant pile of garbage in the foyer and landing on my knees, before crawling the rest of the way out of the house on all fours. My breath comes in ragged gasps as I try to get enough oxygen through the stupid canisters attached to my gas mask. Once I reach the porch, I get back on my feet and run, not stopping until I'm locked in my car with my phone in my hand. Ripping first my gloves off and then my gas mask, I start dialing. I don't even realize who I've called until an operator comes on the line.

"9-1-1, what's your emergency?"

Chapter Six

GREAT. SO NOW I HAVE holes in the walls and ceiling, a dead rat, live mice having a party in the attic, and a $50 fine for calling 9-1-1 for a non-emergency. Thank you, Destiny. Thank you for screwing me over royally. What would you like to do to me next? Have someone steal my car while I'm sitting in it?

I hiss out a sigh of annoyance and frustration. What. The. *Hell*. What am I supposed to do now? It's already four in the afternoon, and I haven't gotten a single thing accomplished, other than moving trash from one end of a room to another. And I'm afraid to go inside the house now, too. That's going to make it kind of difficult to fix it up, I'm pretty sure. Even if I hire subcontractors to do all the work, I still have to inspect what they've done.

I stare out the side window of my car at the front of the house with its ridiculous sagging front porch. And I thought I was going to live inside there by this weekend? Ha. That's a hell of a joke I played on myself. I'm my own worst enemy. What was I thinking buying this rat trap?

All my plans fizzle out like air from a dying, squealing balloon. I've never felt so defeated in my entire life. This project was supposed to get me back on my feet, give me something to occupy my mind and broken heart, but it's turning out to be just one more thing bringing me down. I think the universe is trying to tell me something, and it's not good, whatever it is.

My phone rings and Robinson's name comes up on the screen. All my contacts from my old phone have transferred over, even the ones I didn't want. I press the red key, sending him away. I can't think of anyone I want to talk to less than him right now.

My text alert beeps, telling me someone just left me a message. I click over and look at the screen, knowing full well it's going to be *him* again. Jerk. Baby-stealing, heart-breaking jerk.

Where are you right now? Robinson's text asks.

I consider not answering, but I'm cranky. Being angry at him feels like a great way to express myself and cleanse the bad emotions from my body. It's like therapy in a way.

None of your damn business.

My evil heart sings with happiness. There! That'll show him. He's not a part of my life and he never will be.

I hear you bought a fixer upper.

I stare at my phone, confused and doubly frustrated. How in the hell…? I didn't tell anyone what I was doing. How would he know about the house? This text exchange is supposed to be my mean-girl therapy, not the Robinson-one-upping-me therapy.

Who told you that? I ask. I need to know who I should yell at next.

I glare at my phone, waiting for his answer. Someone's going to get an earful from me about sharing my private business with people like him — baby-stealing snake in the grass.

Your neighbor Rose. Nice lady.

"Dammit, Rose." I never thought to tell her to keep the news to herself. I guess because I never figured Robinson would stoop to spying on me. I'm going to be super-pissed if he slyly interrogated her about me while she innocently served him Earl Grey in her pretty pink teacups. That's practically elder abuse.

My fingers hammer out a new message. *Stop spying on me.*

I'm not spying. Just worried. Can I help?

I laugh out loud in my car. Robinson? Worried about me? Yeah, right. More like worried I'm going to tell James to stop sending him business. And *help* me? The guy never steps out of his front door not in a suit or dressed to kill. If a mouse had landed on *his* head, he'd run screaming into the next county. At least I stopped at my car.

It puffs my ego up a bit to think about it, actually. I'm tougher than he is. I'm tougher than most people when I put my mind to it. I survived a dead rat and a mouse attack, and that's not nothing.

Not sure you could handle it, I say back, smiling at the image I have playing in my head. Maybe I should let him come over here, make him get his hands dirty. That'll teach him to screw me over. Maybe I could even orchestrate a situation where he'd be standing under that hole in the ceiling when a whole pack of mice fell out. I giggle when I picture a tiny mouse running up his pant leg and biting him where the sun don't shine.

Yes, I'm feeling positively evil right now, and I don't care. Evil feels good. It matches the blackness that's swallowing my heart.

Pretty sure I could. He says. *Give me the address.*

I shrug. Fine. He wants to get dirty and covered in mouse poop, who am I to stop him? I will gladly watch him destroy his manicure. After typing out the address, I wait for his reply. This is going to be a beautiful disaster I can't wait to witness.

See you in an hour.

I drop my phone into my purse and turn my ignition halfway so I can listen to some tunes. In sixty minutes, I'm going to be serving up a nice big platter of hot, steaming revenge. My day is finally turning around. Oooohhh yeah, baby. It's all coasting downhill from here.

Chapter Seven

SOMEONE TAPPING ON MY WINDOW wakes me from a cat-nap I fell into waiting for Robinson to arrive. All I can see is a red and blue flannel shirt, a puffy goosedown vest, and jeans. Did a subcontractor see me sitting here and stop to offer help? That would be eerily convenient. Maybe the universe has seen fit to give me a helping hand instead of a smackdown for a change.

I sit up, glancing in my rearview mirror as I move to open my window. There's a black BMW there, the same car that Robinson drives. There's no truck in sight.

When the man bends down and his face shows up in the window, my heart lurches. I can't quite justify my earlier thoughts with what I'm seeing now.

Erp. Does. Not. Compute.

It's a sub-contractor body with Robinson's stupid head on it — same perfectly coiffed hair, same annoyingly straight and blindingly white teeth, same nose with a bump on it, and same chiseled good looks that had me drooling after him for way too long.

I scowl at him as he smiles at me.

"Sleeping on the job?" he asks, winking.

I scowl harder. "Ha, ha. Stop winking at me. Hasn't anyone told you it's weird to wink at women? Next thing you know, you'll be adding the word *Ladies* to the ends of your sentences."

He frowns at me, confused. "What?"

I roll my window up and shove the door open, hoping to catch him in the knees with it. He jumps out of the way, just in time.

"You know. Adding *Ladies* to your sentences. 'How's it going, *ladies*?', 'Can I get you a drink, *ladies*?', 'What's your sign, *ladies*?'" I stand outside my door with my arms folded across my chest for warmth.

"I was always told that asking a woman her sign is passé these days. What's your sign by the way?"

I look away so I don't start smiling at his goofy face. Of course that's what he wants. He thinks he can joke his way past his treachery.

When I know I won't accidentally smile, I look at him again. "My sign is stop. It's a stop sign, Robinson. I thought you were here to help."

"I am." He goes back to his car and opens the trunk. "What exactly do you need help with aside from that porch, the front steps, the bannisters, and the landscaping?"

Front steps? What's wrong with the front steps? I turn around real casual-like, as if I just mean to go into the house, but I eye the stairs carefully. Okay, so some of the boards look a little sad. They could stand being replaced. But that's not an emergency situation, is it?

Robinson quickly catches up with me and meets me at the bottom of the first step. He leans over with a big sledgehammer and drops it on the middle of the second step. It goes right through the wood and buries itself halfway up to the handle.

"What the hell, Robinson!" I turn and glare at him. "You just put a hole in my front steps! You call that helping?" My hands go to my hips. "Would you like to bash in a few of my windows while you're at it?"

He looks at them and nods slightly. "Might be better to keep them in one piece. It'll make them easier to pull out."

"Pull out? Why would I want to pull them out? They're fine."

He shrugs. "I figured since you bought it and planned on living in it for a while you'd want double glazing." He looks at me, waiting for an answer.

Double glazing? What the hell is double glazing? Is that a type of paint?

"You don't know what double glazing is, do you?" He starts to smile again.

"Of course I know what double glazing is." I shove past him, skipping over the second step.

"So what is it, then?" he asks, coming up behind me. We stop at the front door.

"Don't worry about the windows. I have that covered. I need your help with something else." I want to kick myself after the words are out of my mouth. I don't need his help. I don't even *want* his help.

"Okay, what's that?"

"It's inside the house."

He gestures at the front door. "After you."

It pisses me off that he looks so comfortable in those clothes. Since when is Robinson a handy guy? I've been in his office when he's had crews putting up shelves, for God's sake.

I gesture at his flannel. "You have the clothes of a contractor, but how do I know you actually know what you're doing?" I turn around without waiting for his answer and step inside, trying not to flinch at the pile of garbage just inside the entrance. I hate that having him so physically close makes me nervous. I hate him, so why can't I control my pulse? It must be my anger that's making me so jittery. Yeah. I'm going to go with that explanation.

He merely glances at the trash before turning his attention to the living room. "My father was a general contractor. I started following him around on jobs when I was just a kid. Paid my way through college and law school on my construction wages." He moves into the living room and stops in the middle, looking up at the hole in the ceiling.

I'm standing in the foyer, staring at him. "You worked in construction?" I can't see it. He gets a manicure every week. He wears cufflinks. His shoes get shined daily.

He shrugs. "A little." His attention is on the hole. "You probably have rats up there."

"Mice, actually."

He looks at me. "You saw one?"

My smile comes out crooked. "One actually fell on my head."

He takes a quick step to the side. Finally, he's acting more like the Robinson I know, and I can stop entertaining the idea that an alien has taken over his body and transported him over here in a BMW spaceship.

He looks around the room and then toward the kitchen. "Looks like you have your work cut out for you in here." His gaze shifts to me. "Do you know what you're going to do yourself and what you're going to hire out?"

I shrug. "I guess I originally planned to do everything myself. Until that mouse fell on my head."

Robinson laughs, bending backwards in his enthusiasm for it.

My smile disappears.

When he notices, his humor peters out. "Oh, wait. You were serious?"

I hiss out an annoyed breath and go into the kitchen, staring at the spot where I saw that rat. I almost imagine I'll find another one in the same place, as if the little guy I swept across the room is actually a zombie rat and he's going to drag himself back over to his final resting place. I shudder with the idea of reanimated rats. Live ones are bad. Dead ones are bad. Zombie ones? Breaking bad.

I lift my chin, determined not to be cowed into surrendering. "I'll have you know that I bought all the materials today to do that drywall repair, but after finding a dead rat and being attacked by a mouse, I decided to take a little break. You texted me on my break, that's it."

"Caught you at weak moment?" he asks, being way too perceptive for my liking.

"No."

He puts his hand on my shoulder. "Jana, we need to talk."

I tilt my shoulder down to escape his touch and move forward into the connected dining room. "I have nothing to say, and I can't imagine that you do either."

"Oh, I do, believe me." He follows me into the dining room, so I go to the far side of it, looking out the bay window to the ramshackle backyard. What a mess it is. What a mess I am. With Robinson so close, I'm way too jittery. He always could turn my equilibrium upside down and inside out.

"Please, just hear me out." He sounds sad. Enough so, that I'm tempted to turn around. But I don't, because I'll go weak when I need to be strong.

"I really don't care to hear it. Honestly, whatever you say, it's not going to change my feelings or my mind."

"I'd like to try."

I shrug, waiting for the inevitable attempt on his part to erase the un-erasable, horrible thing he's done.

Chapter Eight

YOU STANDING OVER THERE AND me over here in this musty dining room isn't ideal, but I guess it's the best you're going to give me," Robinson says.

I look over my shoulder. "What were you expecting? A candlelit dinner?" That sounds so much like a date I've dreamed a thousand times of having with him, I nearly cringe. But then I control myself by turning around and facing out the windows again. I absolutely hate the fact that I can't be in the same room with him and not think about one of the many times I dreamed of having him as my own. I wasted so many years drooling over him. All I can say is *thank God* I never made my feelings known to him or anyone else. Talk about humiliating. At least now I can walk away with my head held high and not with my tail between my legs.

"No, not a candlelit dinner, but maybe a couple chairs would have been nice." He sighs. "I understand why you're angry with me, I really do."

I laugh bitterly. "That only makes it worse."

"Worse? How so?"

I have to turn around and talk to him now. With that simple admission, he's made me even angrier than before, which I would have thought impossible five seconds ago.

"You understand why I'm angry, and yet you did what you did anyway? That tells me exactly how little you care about me or my feelings." I can't stop this confessional freight train from rolling down the tracks; now that my mouth is open, I can't seem to shut it. "Do you have any idea how that feels for me? To know that this person, who I … admired very much, who I thought was practically a member of my family, completely disregarded my feelings, what was best for me and for someone who I love very much, and just did something completely thoughtless and short-sighted and stupid?" I shake my head at his expressionless face. "No, of course you don't. I don't know why I expected you to care about anything. You don't have the necessary equipment."

"Equipment?"

"A *heart*."

"Come on, now, aren't you being a little harsh?"

"Harsh? *Harsh*?!" I step closer, so very tempted to hit him over the head with something big and heavy. "How could you possibly be this dense? You consider it *harsh* when a woman tells you that you made a mistake taking a child out of her home, out of her arms, and putting that child with a drug addict?" I laugh again. "Man, if you think that was harsh, you haven't heard anything yet."

He holds up his hands in front of him like two stop signs. "Let's dial this down a notch or two so we can work it out. We're not going to get anywhere with you this angry."

"Dial it down. You want me to *dial it down*?" My body is like a pressure cooker right now, and I've reach maximum temperature. I'm about to explode with all the righteous anger that's been building in me for months.

"Maybe just… dial it back?" he says, taking a step to the side.

My eyes follow him and my head swivels slowly on my neck. "So you're telling me to chill out, is that it?" At this point I'm wondering if I'll be able to get that sledgehammer out of my step so I can use it on his car.

He shakes his head, looking worried. "No, that's not what I meant. You're an emotional person, and of course you're going to react emotionally to the things that happen to you."

"Ya think?" I follow him as he backs up into the living room.

"But you need to keep those emotions in perspective. Send them out in the right direction."

"That direction being...?" I tilt my head at him, my voice very calm. Deadly so.

He gives me a weak smile. "Not aimed at me."

I stop walking, shaking my head at him.

"What?" he asks. "Tell me what you're thinking."

I smile, very sad now. Angry-sad. I used to idolize him; he could do no wrong. And yet now, he can do no right. I can't believe I was so blind for so long. "I'm thinking that I used to believe you were so smart, but now I realize you're nothing of the sort."

His head backs up, his chin moving toward his neck. "That's not very nice."

I shrug. "It's a fact. That a man could be so highly educated and yet so clueless, leads me to the conclusion that you are missing something very important in your makeup."

He's starting to look pissed now, which makes me happy. Finally, his mood is matching his inner self.

"What's that? Or should I even ask?"

"It's a *clue*, Robinson. That's what you're missing. You don't have a single clue."

He laughs, but it's not the happy kind. "You're telling me I need to get a clue? What is this? 1998?" He looks over his shoulder at the front door. "Did I just enter the Twilight Zone and not realize it."

"Yeah, Jerk. You entered the Twilight Zone, but it wasn't today. It was the day you made the decision to take Cassie from me. From her happy home. From the place where she was safe, and happy, and with the person who could provide structure and stability for her." The tears have started and they're not going to stop. But since Robinson doesn't have a clue, and probably hasn't since even before 1998, I need to just let him know in no uncertain terms what a horrible lawyer and person he is.

"Did you ever stop to think about Cassie in all this?" I ask. "The fact that she lost her mother, that her father's first reaction to her birth was to *reject* her? The fact that I was the only person willing and able to care for her? And that I didn't just care for her, I *loved* her. I loved her like her own mother would have, had she not been killed in that accident. And you took her away and gave her to my brother. *Jeremy.* The pothead alcoholic who was incidentally also doing crystal meth. But you knew that, I'm sure. James told you everything. But for some crazy reason, you decided a meth addict and his wack-a-doodle artist girlfriend, who he'd *just met* by the way, were better parents for Cassie than me. Than *me*, Robinson." I'm sobbing now, but the words need to be said. I'm not going to stop until they're all out there. His face is falling the more I say and inside I want to sing with glee. Let him feel the pain he's brought me; even just a smidgen of it would bring him to his knees.

"You've known me since I was practically a baby. You know who I am. You *know* I loved her, that I *still* love her with all my heart. After it became clear Jeremy wasn't interested, I let myself fall in love with her, like a mother does when she sees her baby for the first time after her birth." I jab myself in the chest. "*I* was that person. *I* was that mother. And I know I had Laura's blessing. She came to me, you know. She told me I was doing a good job. And Cassie loved me like I was her mother." I want to pull my hair out I'm so frustrated just telling my story. "I was the only mother she ever knew, Robinson! You took her away from her second mother after she had already been taken away from her birth mother once before by a drunk driver! That makes *you* worse! You did it knowingly. *Willingly.* At least that drunk driver was under the influence of something when he did it."

He walks toward me, but I hold my hand out to stop him. "Don't come over here. Don't even come near me. I hate you so much, I'll probably scratch your eyes out."

"But it's not me," he says, speaking in a soft, caring voice, or so he'd have me believe. "I didn't make the decision."

"How can you even say that?!" I scream. "You're the one who did all the legal work! James left it up to you and you made that decision for all of us!" My voice breaks. "For me, for Cassie…"

Robinson is shaking his head. "No, I didn't. The law made the decision. I merely carried out what any other lawyer that Jeremy hired would have."

"Bullshit." I swipe at my tears angrily, pissed I have to be here breaking down in front of this jerk, devastated to be feeling these emotions of abandonment and loss all over again.

"Won't you just hear me out? Just give me five minutes to let me explain?"

I shake my head and point to the door. "No. I'm done listening to you. I've already given you more than you deserve. Way more. Don't ever talk to me again. Leave."

His expression goes dark. "You're being really stubborn right now, Jana, and that's not like you."

I stride toward him and push him toward the door. "You don't know anything about me, Robinson."

He moves along with my insistence, but he doesn't stop talking all the way to the front door. "I've known you for most of your life. You're open and willing to listen. You're not this closed off, angry person, Jana. You're not."

I shove him out onto the porch and grab the door, facing him with tears slashing down my face. "I am now, Robinson. Thanks to you." The pain of that admission breaks my heart all over again. I've changed. I've lost the real me and the only thing left is this angry shell of a woman whose arms are empty where they once held a beautiful baby girl.

After slamming the door, I lean my back on it, sliding down to the floor with the pile of garbage at my feet. I no longer have the strength to stand and cry, and these tears have nowhere else to go but into my lap.

Chapter Nine

I T'S AMAZING, THE POWER BEHIND righteous anger and grief. I guess some people collapse under the weight of it, but me? It gives me wings and fuel to push forward like I've never been able to before. I no longer fear flying mice and rotting rat corpses. I fear nothing. Bring on the zombies, bitches.

By midnight, I have all the garbage that formerly littered the floors of my new house bagged up and out on the front lawn. Tell me I can't fix up this house? Screw you, Robinson. Screw you, World. I can do this, because I *say* I can do this. I might not have any control over my adopted child, but I do have control over this damn house.

I was going to quit for the day when the garbage cleanup was done, but when I realize I still have energy to burn, I decide to tackle the drywall instead. My angry high still hasn't left me, and neither has Robinson's sledgehammer, still buried in the front step. I yank it free, only falling once, and bring it into the house.

With a dust mask on, I start pounding holes in things. My original plan to patch the hole in the wall is out the window, and my new plan to open the space up is on the front burner. Plaster and dust go everywhere as the wood beams, electrical wring, and pipes are slowly revealed. After pounding away for a half hour, I stop and rest on the hammer like it's a cane, admiring my work. I can see the kitchen from the family room now. It's way better this way.

Letting the hammer fall to the floor, I dust my hands off. But when I bend over and try to knock the white powder from my legs, I create a cloud of it around my bottom half. Wow. That's super messy.

Giving up on the clean-up and realizing I've finally run out of anger and energy, I grab my purse and keys and head out the door, locking up behind me. A glance at my phone tells me it's almost one in the morning. Time to rest up for my big day tomorrow. I'm going to knock some holes in some more walls, I think. It's great for getting my mind off *him*.

When I'm safely ensconced in my car, I look at my phone. There are three missed calls from James. I could guess what they say, but instead, I mount my phone on the dash, press the voicemail button, and drive out into the street, headed for my apartment.

The first message was sent probably not long after Robinson left. It plays out over my stereo speakers.

"Jana, this is James. I just got off the phone with Robinson. Would you call me, please?"

I shake my head. Frigging tattletale. Of course he went running to James. What else would he have done? Admitted he made a big, fat, fucking mistake? No, of course not.

The second message plays.

"Jana, James again. Listen, I get that you're upset, but we need to talk about this. I don't think you have the right ideas going on in your head, and I don't want to see you getting so worked up about this stuff. It's not going to help, you know."

Et tu, James? *Et tu*? I'm tempted to grab my phone and throw it out the window again, but the cost of my tantrums is going to cut into my construction budget, so I resist that urge and listen to the last message instead. A female voice comes over the speakers this time.

"Jana, it's Leah. I'm using James's phone. I'm calling to tell you I heard about what happened with Rob today, and I completely and totally get you. I get it, okay? I would feel exactly the same way. You're not crazy and you're not out of line. Can we talk? Call me. But on my phone, not James's phone. I'll be up late. I have heartburn."

I blink a few times, not trusting that the late hour and all my hard work hasn't thrown my hearing off. Did she say she would feel the same way? But Sarah, my brother's new wife and Cassie's new mom, is her best friend. Why would she side with me against her? I play the message again and confirm that she did, in fact, say that.

The relief that flows through me is palpable. It's like someone threw a light on inside the very dark room I've been standing alone in for weeks and hugged me. I have to call her now. I realize as my heart feels lighter that I need the support more than anything in the world.

I search through my contacts at the next red light and press the button that will connect me with Leah's phone. She answers right away in a whisper.

"Hello?"

"Hi, Leah, it's Jana." I'm whispering too.

"What? I can't hear you."

I shake my head at my idiocy and talk in a normal tone of voice. "It's Jana. Calling you back."

"Give me a second," she whispers, "I need to go into the other room."

I hear shuffling and muffled noises before she comes back on the line, no longer whispering. "Okay, that's better."

"Is James asleep?"

"Yep. Sawing logs, one right after the other. I thought his snoring was bad before, but now that I have heartburn, it's worse. There's no hope of me sleeping until at least four when he finally closes his lumber mill down for the night."

"That sucks." I never pictured my brother being that guy who keeps his wife up with his snoring. It's oddly comforting to know he's normal sometimes and not always a superhero.

"Anyway, enough about my petty problems. They're nothing compared to what you're going through. How are you holding up?"

I planned to be strong and confident in this call, showing Leah that I've been wronged in an intellectual and rational way, but that all goes to hell in a hand basket when the tears start flowing again. At this point I'm going to be totally dehydrated before I can get to the water faucet in my kitchen.

"Not good," I finally say. It's all I'm capable of at this point. I still have to get across the Brooklyn Bridge and I can't pull over to cry there.

"I can imagine. Rob came over after he saw you. He said you gave him an earful."

"You could say that."

"He didn't share specifics. At least not while I was in the room. He basically said that you blame him for taking your child from you. That he wrecked a very happy home."

My smile is bitter. "That's about the gist of it."

"Does he know how much you like him?"

My ears start to ring at her question. "*Like* him?"

"Yeah. You know. Does he know you have a massive crush on him? Because if he didn't — and I wouldn't be one bit surprised if he didn't since most men are totally clueless and he's no exception — it would explain why he doesn't quite get the gravity of the situation."

"I'm sorry," I say, somewhat flustered, "but I'm not sure I know what you're talking about."

Leah giggles. "Oh, come on, Jana, don't play. You know you love him. I've seen the way you look at him. And in most of the pictures with you guys in them, you're looking up at him with goo-goo eyes. You're totally crushing on him. Anyone can see it."

"Anyone?" I say, hating how meek I sound.

"Well, not the guys, of course." She snorts. "Totally clueless, every one of 'em."

"I know, right?" I'm relieved to hear her say that. At least that part of her conversation makes sense and doesn't tempt me to hang up the phone. "I told him that today, that he's clueless."

"What did he say to that?" she asks, obviously delighted.

"He told me I time warped him back to 1998."

"Deflection. Classic avoidance technique."

I'm impressed with how clearly she's read the situation without having been there. "That's what I thought too."

"So, what's your next step?" she asks.

"Next step? What do you mean? With the house?"

"No, silly, with Rob."

"There is no next step with Rob. It's over. And I don't even know what *It* was. It was nothing, according to him, so it *is* nothing. Game over. Thanks for playing." I hate that I sound so bitter, but it's real. I am bitter. Bitter, unhappy, sad. Name your negative emotion, that's what I am.

"I don't believe you'll end it that easy."

I turn onto the Brooklyn Bridge, merging in next to a giant double-decker tour bus. "End what, Leah? We weren't a couple. We never went out on a single date."

"Those are just technicalities. You know he was crushing on you too, right?"

That little statement makes my heart stop beating for way too long. I gasp as it starts up again and sends a shock of pain through me. "Where'd you get that crazy idea?" I ask, my voice sounding strange to my own ears.

"Duh. Common sense. I know what a guy looks like when he's trying to picture a girl naked all the time."

My ears go red. "Don't be ridiculous." Him, picture me naked? No way. I hate the surge of heat that moves through me. Traitor body of mine.

"What's so ridiculous about that? You're gorgeous, he's hot, he's straight, which is some kind of miracle considering how good-looking he is, and you've been right there under his nose for, what, like twenty years?"

"Yeah, under his nose like a sister, not a woman he wants to see naked."

Leah laughs. "Like a sister? No. Huh-uh. No man looks at a sister like Rob looks at you. That's illegal in all fifty states."

I can't help but laugh. Leah does have a way with words.

"Listen," she says, "I think I hear James waking up, so I'm going to go now. But let's have lunch tomorrow. Are you free?"

"I'm working on my house all day."

"I'll bring lunch to you, then. We'll have a picnic."

I cringe when I think of her in my place with her big pregnant belly. "That might not be a good idea. It's really dirty right now."

"I'm washable," she says cheerfully. Then she whispers. "Text me the address and I'll see you around 12:30."

I sigh, knowing how persistent she can be when she puts her mind to it. "Fine. See you tomorrow."

"Okay. Bye!"

I take a moment to put the address in a text to Leah at the first stoplight I come too off the bridge. I need to hurry up and get home, so I take off at the next green light and hot-foot it to the apartment. I'm going to need a good night's sleep to have this conversation I know she's planning for tomorrow.

Chapter Ten

THE WEATHER IS TOTAL CRAP, which makes it much easier from a mental perspective to walk into my crap new house. At least I'm escaping the freezing rain and hail. Thankfully, bad weather for construction projects also means several contractors are available to come over and give me bids for the work I need done.

The first guy to show up is the electrician. I give him a tour of the place and stop in the kitchen, giving him my best smile. "So, what do you think? Is this doable?"

He shrugs. "Sure, anything is doable." His round belly doesn't seem to get in his way, even though I'm not sure how he's going to write on the clipboard he's put on the counter. I hope his arms are really long.

He bends over, dipping his belly down so he can write on his three-part form. "I'll work up an estimate for you later today and send it over by email, but at the very least, this is what I recommend you do." He rips off the top copy and gives it to me.

I read through it, making sure I understand. "New wiring, new panel, outdoor…" I look up at him. "There aren't any prices on here. Should that worry me?"

He smiles. "I need to go back to my office and use the computer. Price depends on how many outlets you want, how many rooms, that kind of thing." He taps his head. "The bean's good, but not as good as the computer."

The bean being his brain, I guess. "Okay, well, I look forward to receiving your bid." Shaking his hand, I nod. "I appreciate you coming out so quickly." I only called him two hours ago.

"No problem. Terrible weather makes it easier."

A knock comes at the door and we both walk around the hole I knocked in the wall to see who it is. Another guy dressed in dirty clothes is waiting there for me.

"You must be the plumber," I say, moving forward to shake his hand.

"No, I'm the roofer." He takes my hand and shakes it without a smile. The skin of his palm is like leather.

"Great." I turn my attention to the electrician. "I'll wait to hear from you, then?"

"Yes, indeedy." He nods at the roofer and sees himself out, as I turn my attention to the man with the leather hands.

"So, do you need to actually go up on the roof?"

"Already did." He hands me a piece of paper.

I look down at it and see the price of $30,500 jumping out at me.

"Whoa. That seems a little steep."

He shrugs. "Based on the shape that roof is in, I figured you were going to need the works."

"That bad?" I cringe, waiting for him to reassure me it's probably not.

"Didn't you get an inspection? Can't be that big a surprise."

My heart sinks. "Yes." I remember seeing the inspection report. I didn't pay it too much attention since there was nothing on there that seemed dire enough to warrant not buying the house. His expression makes me think I should have read it more carefully.

"Just let me know if you want us on the job. We could start next week." He begins walking toward the door.

I feel desperate, like I can't just let him walk away without discussing this more first. Thirty thousand dollars? Shouldn't he spend more than thirty seconds explaining his work to me for that much money?

"I'll email you!" I shout as he walks out the door.

"Better call. I'm not much for computers."

The door shuts behind him and I stare at its peeling paint and scratched surface. Not much for computers? What does that even mean? How do you charge thirty grand for a job and not use computers? I think *I'm* living in the Twilight Zone now.

While I wait for the plumber, I busy myself with sweeping up piles of fine, white powder, there courtesy of my hole-making mania of last night. When the doorbell finally rings, an hour after the appointed time, it sounds very sad because the second part of the bell-tone is out of tune. I need to put that on my list of things to replace. The actual list is on the kitchen counter, and it's been getting longer by the minute. Every time I turn around it seems another problem rears its ugly head.

I open the door and smile with my greeting. "Hello."

Well, hell. Finally. A ray of sunshine in my crap day. The plumber is hot. Whoa, like seriously, seriously steamy hot. Should I award jobs based on how cute the owner of the business is? It seems sexist, but I do have to be here all day, so…

"Hi," he says, extending his hand. "I'm Jake."

Of course you are. I shake his hand, my smile growing wider. "Hello, Jake. I'm Jana. Nice to meet you. I assume you're the plumber?"

"That's me." He steps inside after wiping his feet off on the old mat in front. Points for effort, even though it's probably cleaner out on my porch than it is inside at this point.

I'm nervous in the presence of such rough good looks. Is he really a plumber? I might not complain about seeing plumber crack if he's on the job. As my face heats up, I quickly force myself to shift into business mode. I cannot drool over a contractor; he'll charge me double and I'll end up paying it and hating myself for it later when he's long gone.

"So, do you already have an estimate after only walking up to the front of the house like the roofer did, or do you need to actually go through the house?"

He laughs. "Gave you a big price tag, did he?"

I breathe out a sigh of frustration. "I don't know. Is thirty grand big?"

He shrugs. "Depends on the job." His gaze moves to my living room ceiling hole. "Depends on the shape your trusses are in."

I follow his gaze and see another mouse peeping over the edge. "Do mice eat trusses?"

He laughs again. "I don't think so. But you never know until you go up there."

I look at him to see if he's serious, but I can't tell by his expression. It's those green eyes throwing me off. "You must be kidding." The attic? Where the mice have moved in and started throwing parties that get so wild they throw their friends out of holes in the ceilings? No thank you.

"Nope, not kidding. I'll be going up there today for my estimate if you still want one. I could take a look at the trusses for you while I'm up there."

"You could?" I grab his arm I'm so excited about the fact that I don't have to go up there personally.

He smiles. "No problem."

I let him go, worried he'll get annoyed by the fact that I'm probably acting like every other woman who's been caught in his thrall. I'm not that girl. Hot guys don't make me stupid, I swear. My brothers are handsome. Robinson used to be gorgeous by my standards before all I could see was his black heart. I know how to act in the presence of beauty without losing my good sense.

I back away and smile. "I guess I'll leave you to your inspection. Unless you need my help with anything?"

The doorbell rings, singing its sad, tuneless song. I look over my shoulder and then back at him as I wait for his answer.

"No, go ahead. I'll be done in about fifteen minutes or so."

I nod and leave him for the front door where I find Leah standing there with bags in her hands, staring at the porch ceiling.

"You know you have old wasp nests up there, right?"

I look up at the husks of something in both corners connected to the house and shrug. "Par for the course." I move out of the way so she and her belly can enter. "What'd you bring?"

"Sushi for you. Fried rice for me."

"Yum."

She holds her arms out for a hug and pouts. "Give me a hug. I think I need one as much as you do."

I go into her arms willingly, because she's right; I do need a hug. Seeing her reminds me of the fact that I'm about to dredge up the memory of my conversation with Robinson from yesterday, and I'm about as interested in that as I am with having another mouse fall on my head.

Chapter Eleven

WE SIT OUT IN THE back yard at a crappy little card table on two rickety chairs I found in the basement. Leah spreads an old curtain on the top of the table and places a brand new scented candle she bought for me in the center, lighting it with the plumber's borrowed lighter.

"Damn, he's cute," she says, holding the lighter up for emphasis.

"I know, right? Damn." I bite into a hunk of rice and raw salmon.

"You said he's the plumber?"

I nod, swallowing.

"Maybe my pipes need some looking after," she says, looking off into the distance as if she's really contemplating it.

I laugh and nudge her under the table with my foot. "You're bad. James would kick him out."

"Meh," Leah waves me off, "James lets me look. He knows I wouldn't want to be anywhere but with him. Besides … I'm about as unattractive as a woman can get at this point." She rubs her well-rounded belly. "Walking, talking birth control, is what I am."

I bark out a laugh. "No, don't say that. You're beautiful. You're glowing."

She snorts. "That glow? It's sweat, not the fancy fairy dust everyone pretends you practically fart out when you're pregnant."

I choke on my next bite of sushi. "Oh my gob," I say, holding my hand out to catch the falling rice.

"Sorry. Did I say that out loud? Anyway, let's talk about Rob."

I shake my head, throwing the rice I caught out onto the weeds. "No thanks."

"I want to help you move past this, or come up with a game plan."

I shrug, getting angry just thinking about it. "It's just going to take some time. And some more holes in my walls."

"Is that you who put that monster hole in that living room wall?" she asks with a grin.

"Yep, that was me. Last night around midnight."

"You'd better be careful. You don't want to knock down the wrong wall and have the whole ceiling cave in on you. Do you have a hardhat? You should have a hardhat. A pink one. Female power and all that."

"Hmm. That's the one thing I haven't bought yet, I think." I grin at her as she does the same at me.

"I'll get one too," she says. "A purple one."

I lift my soda can at her and clink her bottle of water. "Cheers."

"Here's to safety gear," she says. "And cute plumbers."

"Hot plumbers, you mean," I say, taking a sip of my soda.

A male voice comes from my left. "Excuse me, ladies. Don't mean to disturb, but I have that estimate for you if you're ready."

I choke on my soda when I realize the plumber was standing right there when I declared his sexy-temperature to be hot.

Leah leans over and pats me on the back. "There you go. Easy now."

I hold up a finger in his direction. "Be right there," I say in a hoarse voice.

He disappears inside, the gentleman that he is.

"Oh my god," I whisper, half laughing, half horrified.

"Well, at least there will be no mystery in this relationship," Leah says, smiling and staring off into the distance. "You have to admit ... it's a great how-we-met story."

I slap her hand. "Stop. I have to go in and talk to this guy, and I need to keep a straight face."

She waves me on. "Go ahead. I'm going to eat my fried rice and come up with names for your children." She pauses and then starts again. "Henry... Wilbur... Wolfgang."

"Oh my god," I say, walking up to the back steps, "please tell me James is going to be in charge of naming my nephew." I go inside to the sound of her complaints.

"Hey! I'm a good name picker!"

The plumber is waiting for me in the kitchen. "Here you go," he says, handing me several sheets of paper, acting cool as a cucumber. Maybe he didn't hear me after all. "I can get this to you by email in neater form, but I thought you might want to get your hands on something right away."

Get my hands on something? Yikes. Okay, maybe he did hear me and now he's playing with me. I feel like I'm having a heart attack.

I take the papers from him, nearly yelping when our fingers touch. Did he mean what I think he meant? I glance up at him through my lashes, but he's busy putting his pen away, not looking at me all smoldering and sexy as if he's waiting for me to take him up on some kind of other-than-plumbing offer.

I look down at the paper and the price catches my eye, making me forget all about how sexy this guy is. "Eighteen thousand *dollars*?" I look up, part of me waiting for him to point and me and yell, 'Gotcha!' But instead, he just nods.

"Yep. That's assuming you want a full bath in the master and not just the tub that's there now."

I nod, because yes I do want a full bath in there, but also because nodding is much more polite than crying.

"So, give me a call if you're interested."

This time I could swear I hear something else in his voice, but I don't bother looking up. Eighteen thousand dollar price tags have a tendency to make me lose focus on things like sparkling green eyes and strong jaws.

"Will do," I say, finally looking up to shake his hand. "I'm going to get back to lunch. Can you see yourself out?"

"Sure thing. I look forward to hearing from you." He smiles, lets go of my hand, and walks away, the front door shutting softly behind him.

I'm still staring at the pages of work he's proposed when I walk out into the backyard.

"So, he ask you out?" Leah asks.

I shake my head. "No, but he probably should have before he presented me with this bill." I put it on the table for her to see it.

"Wow, eighteen grand? Does he have to do the entire house over again or what?"

"I guess so." I sit down and stare at my sushi. It's not nearly as appetizing as it was.

"You can get other estimates, but I'll bet they'll be about the same."

I look up at her. "Really? Have you done construction before?"

She shrugs. "Just some stuff at James's place, but I'm looking at what he says he's going to do here," she points at the paper, "and the hourly rate. It doesn't look unreasonable. It's just a big job." She smiles and pushes the paper over to me. "But that's what you wanted, right? That's why you bought this pile of junk instead of a place already put together."

"Hey!" I take the paper and put it next to me. "Pile of junk? That's not nice."

Leah gives me a goofy smile. "Oops. Sorry. Did I just insult your baby?"

The word 'baby' hurts, but I shrug and smile anyway. "Maybe."

"I'm sorry. She's got great bones, this baby of yours. I'm sure when you're done with her, she'll be the prettiest one in the neighborhood."

I laugh. "That's not going to be hard."

"You know what I meant." She tilts her head at me. "What's the problem? Is it the price tag or the fact that it's a lot of work?"

"What do you mean?" I take another bite of my lunch.

"What I mean is, I know you have the money for these estimates. Shoot, you could probably pay to have the thing demolished and a brand new one put up. So what's the problem? Why are the estimates bumming you out?"

I sigh. "I have no idea. Your guess is as good as mine." I throw the last bite of my California roll down on the plastic dish it came in and close the thing up.

"I think this Cassie business is really killing you."

I nod, afraid to try and speak. It *is* killing me. She's right. I feel myself dying inside a little more every day.

"I think it was handled badly."

I want to say something, but I don't trust myself not to insult the man she loves. He was partly to blame. He gave Robinson the green light to make the decision for all of us.

She continues, oblivious to my internal struggle. "But now that it's happened, there's not a lot we can do, but I don't think that means we can do nothing."

I don't want to be so stupid as to hope for something that I know will never be, so I just listen with half an ear. The other part of me is very far away — somewhere where I can't be hurt anymore.

"I think we should all sit down, without Jeremy or Sarah at first, and talk about what happened and what maybe should have happened, and then work from there."

I gather up all my garbage and shove it into the bag it arrived in. "It won't do any good. The past is the past. We all just need to move on."

"I think ignoring things that really hurt you and damaged your relationships with your brothers and Robinson is a very bad idea." She places her hand over mine, stilling my movements. "I see what you're going through. You're miserable and trying to pretend you're okay."

I pull away from her, standing. "That's what I have to do. Fake it until I make it." I start walking to the back door under the guise of needing to clean-up, trying to escape her prying words and attempts at mediating a reconciliation.

"That's not how this kind of thing works," she says, awkwardly trying to follow me, but her chair is not cooperating.

I have to wait for her because she looks so damn pitiful. "Says who?"

She finally stands upright and looks at me, her face flushed. "Says the girl who's intimately familiar with the power of karma, that's who." She clomps through the weeds to my bottom stair, standing just below me. "Just do what I say and nobody will get hurt."

I laugh, knowing she means well, but also fully aware of the fact that I've already been hurt enough. And she can't guarantee my safety any more than my brothers or my attorney could.

"Come over for dinner tomorrow," she suggests. "It's just going to be James and Rob, nobody else."

I shake my head. "I can't."

"Can't or won't?"

I smile weakly. "Take your pick."

She sighs heavily, but comes into the house with me. Thankfully, she takes the hint and lets sleeping dogs lie for the rest of her visit, and I see her off thirty minutes later with a kiss and a promise to stay in touch.

Chapter Twelve

I'M EATING PIZZA WHILE STANDING at the kitchen counter when I hear my front door open.

"Anybody home?" he asks.

Robinson.

I can't believe the nerve of him. He just walks into my house after I told him to get the hell away and never come back? And I thought I locked that damn thing. How did he get in? I must have just left it open. *Damn.* What's wrong with me? This isn't Little House on the Prairie, for God's sake. A gangbanger could walk in here and I'd have to offer him a slice of pepperoni pizza.

I keep chewing my slice, hoping if I'm quiet enough, he'll give up and go away.

I should have known better, though. He comes around the corner and looks startled when he sees me. Then he smiles. "Hey there. I wasn't sure if you were home or not."

"So you just decided to walk in." I keep chewing, even though my food tastes like cardboard now.

"Thought you could use some help. I came dressed to work." He looks down at his flannel and jeans. Even his work boots look like they've seen some action. I hate that he's better at this than I am.

"No thanks. I'm all set."

His gaze drops to the counter where I have all the estimates lined up. All told, I have two roofing estimates, two plumbing ones, three willing electricians, and one landscape guy.

"Wow, you've been busy. Day two, and you already have all these estimates? Good for you."

I want to throw my soda in his face, but I steady my hand in my pocket instead where it can't do any harm. Rationally I know he's just trying to be nice; but I don't want him to pretend to be something he's really, really not.

He walks over to get a better look at my paperwork. "Oh, ouch. That one hurts." He points to my first roofing estimate, fifty percent higher than the second one I received just an hour ago from a guy who actually went up into the attic.

I don't say anything in response. Maybe he'll get the hint and leave if I don't engage in any conversation at all.

"I know this company," he says, pointing to the hot plumber. "They have a great reputation."

I think about the email I got from that guy on my phone just an hour ago. He offered to go over the estimate at dinner. I considered it an offer for a date, not a plumbing job, and I wasn't really interested until I just found out that Robinson knows of him.

"The owner asked me out," I say, hoping it'll make Robinson mad. Maybe Leah's right. Maybe he was harboring a secret crush on me. I almost wish it were true, just so this admission of mine will make him regret something for once.

Robinson shrugs. "I don't know him personally." He looks up. "He a nice guy?"

I shrug too. If he can play it cool, so can I. "Don't know. Just met him. Seems nice enough. Very good-looking."

Robinson's gaze flickers and then he's looking at the estimates again. "So your plan is to open this space up, I take it." He points to something on the plumbing papers. "He's going to re-route all those pipes." His thumb jabs over his shoulder at the wall I ruined. In hindsight, it was probably a bad idea to do that without first having a plan. The plumber, Jake, was kind enough to point this out without making me seem like a complete idiot.

"Yep." I close the pizza box and wipe my hands off on a paper towel. "Listen, I was about to get back to work, so if you don't mind…"

Robinson is back to looking at me and smiling. "Sure. No problem. Where do you want to start?"

"I don't need your help." I grit my teeth together in an effort to hold onto my temper.

"Sure you do. You're just too stubborn to admit it."

"I'm not stubborn, Robinson. I'm actually very flexible and willing to do whatever needs to be done, especially when the shit is hitting the fan and everyone else is falling apart. But you know that about me already, don't you? You don't need me to tell you that."

"How about if I install your new front door lock and handle?"

I left the hardware on the floor in the foyer, intending to watch some videos online to teach myself how to do it.

"That's on my list for tomorrow," I inform him, glancing down at the list from hell that's now onto its third page.

"Great," he says, moving into the other room. "We'll be ahead of schedule, then."

I sigh long and loud, but ultimately decide to leave him to his Good Samaritan work. If he thinks this will earn him forgiveness from me, then he's sorely mistaken. You don't take a child from a woman and then come fix a front door lock and make everything okay. That's not how the world works, and it's definitely not how *I* work.

I pick up my phone and read the email from the plumber again. He seemed really nice. Considerate. He smiled a lot too. Maybe that means he has a great sense of humor, someone I could hang out with and forget my miserable life for a few hours.

I email him back, taking him up on the offer of a dinner to discuss the estimate. What the heck; even if he turns out to be a complete dode, at least I'll learn a lot about plumbing so it won't be a complete loss.

When his positive response and the name of the restaurant come back, I smile to myself. He's got class, too. He shows up to give estimates on time, he offers to explain said estimate to me over dinner, and he suggests a restaurant I only go to for special occasions? Color me impressed. Gee, maybe he's the total package. Maybe he's not the kind of person who would sell a girl out for an hourly rate of five hundred bucks an hour, unlike some people around here.

I keep myself busy taking off cabinet doors in the kitchen that I plan to refinish as Robinson works at the front door. The cold air he's letting in makes the place twice as freezing as it already was, so I put my jacket on. My fingers are frozen by the time he's done and back in the kitchen.

"You should get a space heater," he says, tipping the pizza box lid up.

I climb down from my stepladder and shut the box on his hand.

He looks up with a half-smile. "What? I can't have pizza after laboring for a half hour over your lock?"

When he says it, I realize how petty I'm being, so I let my hand fall away. "Better have done a good job."

He puts half a slice of pizza into his mouth and talks with his mouth full. "Check it out." He uses his food to point toward the door.

I walk away with my chin up. It better be perfect or I'm going to insist he take it all apart. I'm actually looking forward to it. Maybe if I humiliate him, he'll finally get the hint and stop coming around.

Unfortunately, the lock has been installed perfectly. It moves like it's been greased with butter, and the new handle appears to be exactly level. Even after watching three how-to videos on my phone and reading the ridiculously complicated instructions, I was still very much in the dark about how to install it, but he just walked in and did it without a single request for help. I wanted him to be Mister Screwup so I could kick him out of here for good, but it turns out he's Mister Fixit. *Dammit*. Why do all of my hopes fall to shit where he's concerned?

"What's next?" he asks from behind me.

I sigh and my shoulders sag as my chin rests on my chest. I feel totally and utterly defeated. Nothing, and I mean nothing, is working out in my favor. It seems stupid that I wished for this lock installation to fall flat when it's my own home he's helping repair, but I can't change how I feel. It's like the entire universe hates me. When I want something to go well, it goes bad. When I want something to go bad, it goes well. Every day is opposite day.

"Nothing," I finally answer. "There's nothing next." Tears make my eyes sting.

Robinson steps closer. "Don't say that. You have a list a mile long in there. Let me help lighten your load. I can build things, fix things…"

I can't look at him, so I stare at the floor, my back to him and all his good intentions. "Rob… I just can't. You can't fix things. I can't do this." I've heard of heart-ache before, but never realized it's such a literal thing. My chest is actually throbbing with pain. Every beat is like a knife stabbing me in between my ribs.

His hand on my shoulder pulls me around and then his finger on my chin lifts my eyes to his.

"You have to let me back in, Jana."

I shake my head. "No. You're out. You're out for good. I wish you'd just accept that and move on."

"But why?" His voice is full of anguish. "What did I do that's so unforgivable? And don't say that I took Cassie from you, because I didn't."

"I can't believe you really think that." I shake my head, so confused about how a man so smart can be so incredibly dense.

"You need to let me tell you what really happened."

"I know what really happened. I was there. Believe me, I'll never forget."

"No, you weren't there. You were in here." He points to my head. "And in here." He points to my heart.

I want to smack his finger away, but I don't. I just listen, a ringing in my ears making it difficult to hear too well.

"The law says that the court must do what's in the best interest of the child…"

I open my mouth to argue about how putting a child with a drug addict could never be in her best interests, but he holds up his hand to shush me.

"…Just let me finish." He takes a deep breath and continues. "As I said, it's the best interests of the child they look at. And almost without exception, unless the parent is truly incapacitated, the best interest of a child is to be with a birth parent who is willing and able to care for her."

I open my mouth again, but he just keeps on talking right over me.

"Jeremy got his shit together. He was and is still going to AA meetings. With Sarah there to support him, he was turning his life around. It was only a matter of time before he hired someone *you don't know* and got Cassie back. It would have been a stranger who didn't care about you, and I couldn't stomach the idea of that happening. I knew you were going to be crushed. I knew how much you loved her."

"Don't say it in the past tense, as if I don't *still* love her like my own daughter," I say, nearly choking on my tears.

"I didn't mean it that way and you know it." He takes my arms and shakes me a tiny bit. "Jana, I know you. I know you so well. I've been in your life for what seems like forever. You're family to me. I'd never do anything to you with malice or negligence. You have to believe me. I had your best interests at heart."

I pull myself out of his grip and take a step back. "How can you say that? You took my daughter from me."

"No." He frowns, taking a step toward me and holding my arms firmly. "She is *not* your daughter. She's Jeremy's daughter. You cared for her when he was lost, but that didn't change the fact that he has the right to raise her." His voice softens. "Just as you have the right to raise your own children one day." He pulls me against him and talks over my head. I'm too weak to fight him as his words slice through me and cut me to the bone. "Imagine if you had a daughter one day and then something terrible happened to your health and you couldn't care for her for a year. And your brother took her in. Wouldn't you want her back after you were healthy again? Would you ever agree to let him keep her, as much as he loved her and took care of her when you couldn't?"

He's painting a picture I don't want to see. I try to fight him, but he holds me tighter.

"Please, Jana. Please…"

"No!" I shout, finally succeeding in pushing him away. "I don't want to hear anything else from you!" I point to the door, breathing like I just ran a mile. "Get out! Just get out!"

"You know I'm right!" he shouts back, his face dark red.

"Get out!" I screech, no longer sounding human.

He strides to the door, grabbing his toolbox from the ground. "You're hurting everyone with your attitude," he growls as he yanks the door open. His glare carries an anger I've never seen from him before. I think he's finally starting to hate me back, and it should make me happy but it breaks my heart all over again.

"Shut up! I don't want to hear anything else from you!" I feel like I'm being torn apart, as if Robinson's pulling my skin from my bones. My head is on fire and a headache rages inside my skull. Sobs mix with my words and make them sound unhinged. "Get out! Get out! Get *out!*"

"I'm leaving. And I won't be back." He walks over the threshold and shuts the door behind him.

"Good!" I scream. "That's what I want!"

I crumble to the floor when I realize that I'm lying through my teeth and crushing my own soul all over again.

Chapter Thirteen

I DON'T KNOW WHAT I would have done all week without all those Youtube videos to guide me through the process of repairing little things around the house, to help me understand what the heck people are talking about when they use words like cantilever, sistering, change order, and pitch, and to teach me about the use of feng shui in laying out the rooms and placement of windows. Now, after a week has passed, I really feel like I'm on the right track for getting this house remodeled in style. Even though my heart's a mess, my life is looking up.

I'm glad it's Saturday night, my big work date with Jake the plumber finally here. I plan to drink copious amounts of wine, and if the estimate looks good, I might even kiss him goodnight. A reward for a job well done.

He picks me up at my apartment on time, looking adorable in grey slacks and a black sweater. He pushes the sleeves up inside my warm living room and reveals the strong forearms that are clear evidence of the hard work he does all week.

Normally I'd go ga-ga over hands like his, wide and well-veined, sprinkled with wiry hair, but all I can think about is Robinson's stupid fingers. I always saw them as paper-pushers, but after he came over and worked on my locks, I imagined them as something else for the first time ever. I hate to say it, but he became more manly to me that night — right before I kicked him out of my life forever.

Figures. And he's done exactly what I asked him to do too, namely, never contact me again. I should be happy about it, but it's eating me up inside. It makes me hate him *and* me when I should be completely satisfied with the outcome.

"Nice place," Jake says, his gaze roaming the room. "Not sure why you'd want to leave it for the other one." He smiles, so I can't tell if he's kidding or not.

"The other one will be great too. Eventually."

He nods. "I have no doubt."

I take his words as a compliment and smile back. "You ready?" I'm wearing my little black dress, guaranteed to turn heads.

"Definitely. Been looking forward to it."

My face feels a little warm at his admission. Isn't he supposed to be playing hard to get? Planning for at least three days of not calling me after the night is over? It's been a while since I've gone out on a date-date, but I'm pretty sure the rules haven't changed.

"Me too," I say, going for full honesty. Might as well skip the games. We're both single, unattached, and looking for a good time. Why play it any differently?

He and I walk to the elevator together and then down to the street, stopping just outside the front doors. Jake leaves me there, stepping over to the curb and flagging down a cab. I wait for him to open my door before getting in and sliding over.

"One If…, on Barrow," Jake says, waiting to be sure the cabbie knows what he's talking about. The older man nods without a word, and off we go into the sea of cars starting to build as the night gets later. We'll have a hard time finding a cab when we're done, so I'm glad I wore my wool coat and matching fluffy cashmere scarf and hat.

"You've eaten at One If By Land before?"

"Yes. Have you?"

He nods. "Once or twice."

I smile a little, imagining all the single women needing plumbing work he's probably taken there. I'm sure I'm not the only one he's offered to go over an estimate with like this.

He grins too, one side of his mouth going up more than the other. It's very charming. "What's that devious smile for?" he asks, nudging me.

I look out the window for a second and then back at him. "Not devious. Just wondering how many other potential clients you've brought there."

"None." He winks at me. "I promise."

"But you've been before, right? Who'd you go with?" From what I remember, it's a romantic restaurant, not really one for a business meeting, so naturally I'm thinking this is his lair. I'll bet he has women drooling over him all the time. If it hadn't been for Robinson ruining my week, I'd probably be doing the same thing right now. Jake's hot, he's a great dresser, his hair is amazing, and those eyes of his are just stunning. But all I can think about is the BMW I didn't get to mangle with the sledgehammer and how smoothly that stupid lock keeps working on my front door.

Jake purses his lips as he considers my question. "Hmmm, let's see... who did I take there last?" He comes back to me and smiles. "My mother. It was her birthday."

I laugh, thinking he's kidding me.

"What? Why's that funny?"

I stop laughing, feeling self-conscious. "You're not joking? Oh. Sorry."

He smiles. "Yeah, I was kidding. I wouldn't take my mother there. Talk about awkward."

I nudge him in the leg. "Tease."

We don't talk the rest of the way there about anything of substance. I'm happy to chat about the weather and the problems with potholes getting bigger on the roads until we reach the restaurant. It takes the pressure off the reason why we're even in this cab together. I feel kind of funny now that I'm out here with him. Why did I agree to go out on a date with my plumber? I'm not sure now. I think it's Robinson's fault. Everything's his fault.

He opens my door for me and helps me out of the cab at the curb. I try not to be too obvious as I watch to see how much he tips the driver. Thankfully, he does a good job, not being a cheapskate, unlike more than half the men I've dated. I have this thing about tipping people; I think anyone who works for tips should get great ones, especially if the service is decent. It's how I'd feel if I'd ever worked for them. Retail's bad enough, but driving cabs and waiting tables? I can't imagine anything more awful; people can be so horrible when they're being waited on. There are many women I would have loved to lock in the dressing rooms when I worked in women's clothing boutiques.

The warmth of the restaurant spills out over us as the doors are opened from the inside. The brick building and large archway welcome us inside like old friends. I don't know what's going to happen tonight with Jake, but at least it's going to happen in a lovely place. He places his hand on my lower back and guides me to the reception desk and several heads turn to watch us walk by.

Chapter Fourteen

WELCOME," AN EMPLOYEE OF *ONE If By Land, Two If By Sea* says, smiling and gesturing for me to continue in.

"Thank you." I smile my way through the front reception area, appreciating the ambiance and décor. It's even more romantic than I remembered. My coat, scarf, and hat are taken and we're led to our table, a nice and somewhat private spot on the far side of the room.

Next to us on the wall is a tall painting of a man wearing a red cloak, sitting in a formal chair. I have the strangest sensation that he's watching me and that he's prepared to listen to everything I say. It compels me to speak in a whisper when Jake asks me if this table is all right.

"Yes," I say, leaning toward him as far as I can. My boobs are resting on the linen napkin and silverware in front of me.

He looks to the right, out at the rest of the tables, some of which already have diners at them.

"Why are you whispering?" he says in a really low voice.

My eyes are drawn up to the man in the cloak. "I'm not sure."

Jake follows my gaze and then looks back at me, smiling. "It does kind of feel like he's eavesdropping, doesn't it?"

"I know, right?" I grin.

Jake raises a finger at the nearest waiter.

I grab it and push it down on the table. "No, don't." I giggle.

"What?" He's smiling. "You don't want to move?"

I shake my head, pleased that he'd be a pain in the butt and insist on a new table just to make me feel better.

"I'll have him take the picture down, then." He tries to lift his finger again, but I push it down to keep it on the table.

"No. Leave Sylvester where he is."

"Sylvester?" Jake looks up at the painting. "Hmmm, he does look like a Sylvester, you're right."

I let my hand slide away from his and use it to put my napkin in my lap. I don't feel nearly as self-conscious as I did when he first picked me up. Now that we're being silly and laughing together, this feels less like a date and more like hanging out with a friend.

So far, Jake seems like he could be a pretty good one — a friend, that is. I should probably be imagining him naked right now, but it's just not there for me. I'm more interested in what he's going to do with my kitchen pipes, which makes me think I need to get some alcohol in me. A guy this handsome and funny deserves some drooling over. Maybe I just need to kickstart the process or something.

"So, are you seeing anybody?" he asks, looking right at me.

My mouth kind of drops open as I try to justify what I was just thinking against what he just said. He's obviously not thinking friendship like I am. Oh boy.

His confident expression slips. "Too obvious? Sorry, I should have just tried to figure it out through conversation."

I laugh. "And how does someone do that?" I like that his sense of humor keeps pushing us through the awkward moments.

He shrugs. "I don't know. Probably... first I'd ask you what you did recently that was a lot of fun. Act like I'm just bringing up interesting conversation starters when what I'm really doing is delving into your personal life."

I nod, getting the idea. Pretty ingenious, actually.

He continues. "And if you said, 'Oh, my boyfriend and I, blah, blah, blah,' then I'd have my answer."

"What if I said, 'My best friend and I went to the zoo.'?"

He nods, one of his eyebrows going up. "Okay, a challenge. I get it." A pensive look covers his face for a few seconds before he looks at me again. Now he reminds me of Sherlock Holmes the way he's focusing. "All right, so you and your *friend* you say? Well of course then I'd have to figure out if this friend is male, female, or canine."

"Canine?" I laugh, reaching for my glass of water just provided by a silent server who's already disappeared.

"Sure. Man's best friend. You could have one of those purse-dogs you carry around with you; you never know these days."

My face is getting a cramp from smiling so much. "Okay, so ask me. Figure out if it's a male, female, or canine."

He smoothes down the front of his shirt and then puts on his cool expression. "Oh, the zoo. Love the zoo. Was it your friend's idea to visit or yours?" He waits for me to smile, and I do.

"So with this question you eliminate the canine."

"Exactly." He takes a sip of his water. "And your answer?"

"My answer is that it was my idea to go to the zoo."

He frowns. "Dammit. Foiled again."

I laugh, leaning back in my chair. "Keep going. I want to see how long this takes you."

"Careful," he says. "I love a challenge."

I shrug, trying not to believe that he means that in a romantic way. But it's hard to deny how well we get along. I just wish I knew why I feel the urge to snuggle up and drink hot chocolate with him instead of strip him naked and chase him around my bedroom. It's not like me to be this puritan.

He steeples his fingers in front of his chest. "Okay, so at the zoo, did you go to the restaurant there? I hear it's pretty good."

"And they also don't allow dogs inside," I say, nodding out of respect. "Good one. My answer is… no. We didn't visit the restaurant."

He shakes his head. "You're difficult. I like it."

I don't smile. "Do you give up?"

"Never." His expression goes serious. "What'd you do after the zoo?"

I get serious too. "We went for ice cream in the park."

"What flavors did you get?"

"I got chocolate. My friend got vanilla."

"A-ha!" he says, his finger pointing to the ceiling. "Your friend is *not* a dog, and whoever it is, male or female human, they are boring!" He shakes his head in disappointment for my poor, fake best friend. "Vanilla."

A server stops at our table and hands each of us a menu, interrupting the interrogation. I stifle a giggle at how goofy Jake must have looked when the guy walked up.

"Thank you," Jake says to the server, before looking at me and rolling his eyes around.

I hide behind my menu, peeking over the top at him.

He leans toward me, speaking low. "And after the ice cream?"

I lower my menu and lean over it. "We went shopping."

His eyes sparkle. "Bingo. What did you shop for?"

"A coffee machine."

He scowls. "Now you're just being difficult."

I laugh. "Okay, so I shopped for a new purse."

He leans back and shrugs. "Okay, I'm good then. You either shopped with a girlfriend or he's gay."

"You wouldn't shop for a purse with me?" I say it all cutesy, and realize too late I'm seriously flirting.

"I would." It's all he says, but I know what he means. He likes me.

It would be a mistake to keep flirting with him when the romantic flow is so one-sided. I sigh really long and open the menu.

"Oh no."

I look up at him. "What's the matter?"

He's looking at his menu too. "I don't like the sound of that sigh."

I shake my head. "Ignore me. I'm having a bad week."

"Next week will be better," he says with confidence.

"Says who? You?"

"It's all just a state of mind," he says.

"Is that so?" It makes me kind of cranky to have someone who I recognize as at least fairly intelligent act like my life is something I can just decide is awesome and it will be. Nothing I say to myself in front of the mirror is going to change what Robinson did or what Jeremy and James did either. I wish it could be that easy.

"Sure. Don't you believe that?" He looks serious.

"Some things are not under my control, and those things can really be awful. The power of positive thinking or whatever you're talking about isn't going to change any of that."

He shrugs and goes back to his menu. "Everything is in your control. I can teach you about it later, but right now, I need your help." He's frowning at the menu.

I ignore his offer of help because I'm quite sure a plumber does not have a magic wand he can wave over my life and fix everything wrong with it. Instead, I focus on his request.

"Help? With what?"

"Please tell me what mushroom kaboocha ravioli and salsify kale is."

I locate the menu item he's talking about, sure I'll be able to help him, and then frown. That's really all it says.

"Is salsify kale a type of kale or are they salsifying the kale?" he asks.

"I have no idea." I laugh, shaking my head. "What is up with these restaurants trying to trick us into eating kale anyway?"

He drops his menu to the table and gestures at me. "Thank you."

"What?" I look up, mystified.

He leans in and whispers. "If you'd ordered kale for dinner, I was never going to call you again."

Now I can't stop laughing. "Really? But what if I wanted to hire you as my plumber?" My smile cramps are back.

He shakes his head. "I would have turned you down. A man has to draw the line somewhere."

"And you draw it at kale-eaters?"

"A man's got to do what a man's got to do."

I lower my menu to the table and give him the sly-eye. "I sense a story here."

He smiles and picks up his menu, shrugging as if he's ready to play hard to get. "I'll tell you mine if you tell me yours."

Chapter Fifteen

THERE'S NO TIME FOR US to share our secrets at the table. The servers are there bringing us appetizers, wine, food, coffee, and then the bill. Conversation during the first course turns to the estimate he gave me, and he goes over it, line by line, explaining the whys and wherefores of the whole thing. By the time we get to our coffee, I completely understand every single bit of work he thinks should be done, and I'm absolutely convinced he's the man for the job.

"You're hired," I say as the cab pulls up in front of my apartment. "In case you hadn't figure that out yet."

He turns to me and smiles, holding out a hand to shake.

I take it in my gloved hand and smile back. "See you next week?"

"Sure. But I could come up for a drink now if you want."

I lean in and kiss him on the cheek. "Not this time. Maybe some other night."

He kisses me too, and the shadow of his beard lightly grazes my cheek as he pulls away, leaving a shiver to follow behind. I'm seriously tempted to invite him up, but know in my heart it would be a mistake. I'm too much of an emotional wreck to handle good sex right now. Or bad sex for that matter, but I don't think he's capable of the bad kind. He's been too on-the-money all night for that. He's proven himself to be thoughtful, creative, funny, sexy, smart, and downright nice. I'm sure the sex would be amazing.

I frown as I'm opening the back door, turning to face him for just one more question. "Why exactly are you single again?" I ask.

He smiles, but the expression's not as easy to come as the others he's shared tonight. "Everyone has a story. Maybe someday I'll tell you mine."

"Deal." I leave him at the curb and watch the cab as it drives away. I sigh when I realize that I probably should have invited him up. I have no reason to lock myself away like a nun. It's not like I have other prospects out there waiting for me. It seems like I can't make a decent decision to save my life.

"There you are," says a voice from behind me.

I spin around at the familiar tone, my good mood dissipating into the freezing night air.

"What are you doing here?" I demand to know, pissed and not hiding it.

Robinson is standing there in a wool overcoat, steam from his breath floating around his face.

"Are you following me?" My voice has a hysterical edge to it. I just can't handle the fact that I had a nice evening with a great guy and then here *he* is to screw it all up, right before I'm going to go to sleep. Now, thanks to him, I'm probably going to have nightmares about Cassie being stolen away when I might have managed a sexy dream with Jake as the star actor.

"No, of course not. I stopped by to see if I could talk you into going out for a drink with me."

I cross my arms over my chest and just stare at him.

"What?" he asks, innocently as if he doesn't know what I'm thinking — the same thing anyone in my shoes would be thinking about him just stopping by after I've told him to go to hell.

"I'm just trying to figure out if you really are that clueless."

"I think we already discussed the status of my clue-having before, didn't we?"

"Oh shut up." I walk briskly toward the door to my building.

"Does that mean you don't want to get a drink?"

"Not with you." I punch in the code to unlock the door. Dammit, why didn't I invite Jake up? That would have been awesome, letting Robinson see that. Maybe then he'd finally leave me alone.

"And not with that guy who just dropped you off, I guess."

I spin around and glare at him. "Stay out of my business."

"I can't, Jana, I'm worried about you."

"Yes, you most certainly *can*." I yank the door open and stand there blocking his way. "You're not coming in."

"Not even for a cup of coffee?"

"No!" I can't believe the nerve of him. Since when has Robinson been so bull-headed anyway? I don't remember him being anything but amenable in the past.

"I have some news for you. About Cassie."

My arm slips from the door and my face falls. "Oh, so you're the go-between now? Between Jeremy and me? My own brother doesn't even want to talk to me about the baby I raised for him for almost an entire year?" Tears take the place of indignation, but I can't help it. It's like another knife's been shoved between my shoulder blades.

"No, no, nothing like that. I said that wrong. Please don't think that. It has nothing to do with me being a go-between."

I'm back to being angry. "You're making no sense, Robinson. I think you need to leave."

"It's because I'm exhausted. I've been up all night for a week. I haven't slept at all. I can't get our last conversation out of my head."

"Then the last thing you need is coffee." I step into the foyer and try to shut the door.

He moves up and puts his foot in the way. "Please? Can I just come up for a couple minutes? I promise I'll leave when you want me to."

I look down at his foot. "Why do I find that so hard to believe, I wonder?"

He pulls his foot back and stares at me, pleading with his expression.

I let the door shut and talk to him through the glass. "Go home, Rob. I have nothing left to say to you."

"Is he your new boyfriend?" he asks as I'm turning around.

I pause, turning back to look at him. "Who?"

"That guy in the cab."

I point at his face through the glass. "You sound like a stalker. Cut it out."

He holds up his hands and backs up. "I know. That's terrible. I take it back. I'm sorry. I'm just... I don't know what the hell I'm doing anymore." He drops his head and turns away, walking down the sidewalk away from my building.

I stand in the foyer and chew my lip. I should just let him go, I know that. But this isn't just some guy. This is Robinson. I wanted to deny it before when he staked his claim, but he wasn't lying or just wishful thinking when he said he's one of the family. He's been to every Thanksgiving, Easter, and Christmas dinner we've had since he was eighteen years old. I grew up thinking I had three big brothers, one of whom I had a very unhealthy crush on. He's helped James out of I don't know how many issues that have cropped up with his medical practice and the inevitable liabilities that come with rearranging people's faces. And when he told me about Cassie, about why he did what he did giving her back to Jeremy, there was that tiny, niggling thought in the back of my head that he was right about one thing: if I ever have a daughter and then can't care for her, no way in hell will I just walk away and let her temporary caregiver keep her when I'm better again. Nothing else he said made sense to me, but that did. My heart spasms painfully at the thought that I'll never see Robinson again, that he'll listen to me when I tell him to stay the hell away forever.

I push through the door and run down the street after him. "Robinson! Wait!"

A cab two blocks ahead pulls away from the curb, leaving a trail of exhaust smoke behind it. It's quickly swallowed up by all the other cabs swarming over the streets of Manhattan, leaving the sidewalk empty. I slow to a walk and then stop when I realize that Robinson is in the backseat, and the cab's brake lights aren't going on.

Chapter Sixteen

THE NEXT FEW DAYS FLY by, and I'm happy for all the distraction my house renovation is providing. I haven't moved into my new place yet, but I can see it happening in another week or two. Jake doesn't disappoint either. He shows up on time with three guys working for him, and they go to town on my plumbing without stopping except for lunch, every day. They eat on the job site and then go right back to work until six o'clock, poking holes in walls, running pipes, soldering, and God knows what else. I just try to stay out of their way.

I keep expecting Robinson to call me and explain himself or apologize, but my cell phone remains free of his number popping up. Leah calls me daily to see how everything's going and to find out how I'm feeling. James called once and left me a message, but I haven't called him back. I don't know how much Robinson is sharing with him right now, but I don't want to have to apologize to him for my behavior. I'm not ready to admit I've done anything wrong. So what if Robinson's feelings were hurt? He deserves it. My moment of weakness as he drove away was easy to understand. He'd looked so pitiful. But after I had a good night's sleep, I realized it doesn't matter how pitiful he looks; he's not the man for me. Not anymore.

"Penny for your thoughts," Jake says from off to the side.

I turn to look at him and smile, walking over to wipe the black smudge from his cheek.

"I've got schmutz?" he asks, taking a rag out of his pocket and swiping it across his cheek.

"Yeah. You had schmutz, but I got you covered."

"Thanks, you're a pal."

I feel kind of bad about the pal moniker, but he's right. We are pals. It makes me even more curious about why he doesn't have a girlfriend. Does he have a problem with other women finding him adorable in an older brother kind of way?

"Doing anything fun this weekend?" I ask casually.

He leans back and barks out a laugh.

My face goes a little red. "What? Did I say something funny?"

"You're using my moves on me. Did you think I wouldn't notice?"

I throw a piece of bent wire at him that's sitting randomly on my counter. "Shut up, I was just being friendly."

He leans on the counter. "Okay, I'll bite." He readjusts his expression. "Yes, in fact, I am doing something fun this weekend."

"Oh, really?" I nod, acting like we're just having a conversation. "And what might that be?"

"Well, a friend of mine and I are planning on going to Central Park to throw a frisbee around."

My eyebrows go up. "Isn't it a little cold to be throwing a frisbee around in the park?"

He shrugs. "No snow. We're tough."

I smile all evil-like. "So I know your friend is either a guy or a dog."

He chuckles. "Or a hardcore chick who doesn't mind freezing her buns off to spend the day with me."

"You have a point."

"Would you like to join us?" He bites his lip for a second and I have to laugh.

"Oh, man, you're bad."

"What?" he acts all innocent when we both know he's not.

"Now I'm screwed."

"How so?" He takes a step toward me.

"Because. Unless I ask for details, I could be accepting an invitation to a doggy frisbee throwing date or a sexy threesome."

"Hmm... a threesome?"

I gesture out into the room. "Yeah, your friend could be an electrician or that hardcore chick you mentioned."

"Sounds kinky," he says, stopping just next to me.

I look up at him and his sparkling green eyes. "Do you have a dog?" I'm trying really hard not to smile.

"Yes, I do."

"And does he like to play frisbee in the park?"

"Yes, he does. He's a border collie and he lives to play."

"Why don't you bring him to work with you?"

"Because he prefers to stay home with my wife."

My heart drops into my stomach and I stare at him as the blood leaves my face.

He smiles. "I'm just kidding. I'm not married."

I punch him right in the stomach, and he doubles over as the air whooshes out of him.

"Holy shit," he grunts out. "You pack a hell of a punch."

"Oh my god," I say, laughing, still incredulous over his answer and the fact that I just gut-punched him.

Who does that? Who socks her sub-contractor in the belly? I haven't done it to anyone but my brothers, and the last time I did it was probably ten years ago. But my plumber? Seriously?

He puts his hand on the counter and tries to stand, but he stops partway and just looks at me. "Totally got what I deserved."

"Yes, you did." I fold my arms over my chest and try like hell to control my reaction. I should *not* laugh at physically assaulting the man who still hasn't finished plumbing my house.

"But at least now I know you were hoping I'm single."

I shake my head. "You really need to get professional help."

"How about I just come over to your place, lie on your couch, and tell you all my problems?"

"When?" I ask, ready to take his challenge and meet him head on.

"Tonight."

I shrug, moving out of the kitchen to go back to my dry wall repair. "Fine. See you at eight."

"I'll bring dinner!" he shouts from the kitchen.

I cross the creaky floorboards to the master bedroom. "Indian!" I shout back.

"You got it!"

I smile for the next hour as I picture playing therapist to the hottest plumber in Manhattan. I only lose that smile when I imagine Robinson showing up outside my door and spooking the guy off.

I take out my cell and send him a text, just to be sure. I don't even think twice about doing it. He has some kind of crazy radar that goes off anytime I'm with another guy.

I hope you don't plan on any more dropbys. I'm allowed to have a life without you in it, you know.

He doesn't answer, and I stew over it all day long and straight into the evening. Ten minutes before Jake is scheduled to arrive at my apartment, I sneak downstairs and look out the doors of my building, fully expecting Robinson to be hiding in the shadows. But he's not there, and the street looks totally empty, save for the cabs that drive by from time to time and slow when they see me standing there. I walk back into my elevator, for some reason feeling very alone. Why didn't he text me back? Is he really that over me that he can ignore my instructions not to bother me? I feel like I'm in high school again, playing teenage games. Maybe tonight I should lie on the couch and tell Jake all my problems instead of the other way around.

I send a text to my brother James as I ride the elevator back up to my apartment. When I'm in the hallway it goes out.

Is Rob okay? Haven't heard from him in a while.

Two minutes later, I get a response.

Better to just leave it alone.

My heart crumbles in on itself, and I feel the insane urge to bawl like a baby. Stepping into my apartment, I slam the door behind me. I guess everyone knows what a horrible bitch I am now. Even my own brother is telling me to stay away, as if I'm the one who's the bad influence.

Why is my own family against me? I'm not the one who did anything wrong. If anything, I'm the only one who did anything right. James was hardly there when Cassie was born. I had to practically force him to take her overnight, and he only did it because he felt guilty. After that, it was Leah who always offered. So why do I feel so horrible about Robinson being okay with staying away and my brother telling me to back off? It was my idea, for chrissake. Ugh, I hate being this confused inside my own head.

The buzzer goes off in the front entrance of my apartment, distracting me from my inner rant. I go over and press the button.

"Hello?"

"It's your friendly neighborhood plumber, here for intensive couch therapy."

I press the button, trying to muster up a smile for a guy who deserves none of my bitchy mood. "Come on up."

I hear the door click and lift my finger from the button. Time to put on my happy face and get through this night with my heart in one piece.

Chapter Seventeen

JAKE ARRIVES WITH A BAG in each hand and a giant smile. It only slips a little when he sees my expression.

"Best Indian food in Manhattan, delivered hot to your doorstep."

I open the door farther and gesture for him to come in. "You can put the bags right on the table."

He leans in and kisses me on the cheek before he continues on into the apartment. I try to act like it's totally natural and casual, but it takes me by surprise. It's kind of strange to see him bent over my kitchen sink during the day and bringing me dinner with a kiss at night. It's not entirely unpleasant… just weird. It's like we're a couple, but we're not.

We should be; I mean, it totally makes sense on paper. He's hot and gainfully employed with a great reputation. I'm single and looking. He's obviously interested. I *should* be interested. So what's wrong with me? Why the hesitation? Why all the awkwardness every time we're together in a semi-romantic situation? I don't have this problem with him on the job site. We work together all day long without a single heart flutter. I joke around with him like we know each other way more than we do. But when we're alone and he kisses my cheek, I start wanting to hide in the closet. I'm definitely the one who needs some couch therapy.

He unpacks the food while I take out and uncork a bottle of wine.

"I wasn't sure if you like your food spicy, so I told the chef to give it to us half and half."

"Good choice. But I do like it spicy so…"

He finishes the sentence for me. "Next time I'll kick it up a notch."

I smile, happy about the idea of another meal with him. He is so damn easy on the eyes. Tonight he's wearing designer jeans and a university sweatshirt that makes him look ten years younger. I'll bet he was the hottest guy in his entire class. It makes me wonder again why his best friend is a dog and not a woman.

"Did you go there?" I ask, pointing at the Fighting Irish mascot on the front. "Notre Dame?"

"Sure did. Played basketball there too."

"You did? Huh." Now that I think about it, he does look pretty athletic. Broad shoulders. Tall enough to be a point guard. Robinson was on the crew team at school. He was always so lean.

My hands freeze as I realize I'm comparing Jake to Robinson, as if Jake has to measure up to him — to the guy I told to go away and never come back, and then started missing when he followed my instructions.

I walk over and put my hand on Jake's shoulder. I need to put an end to this craziness and now. It's time for me to move on and leave the past behind.

He stops moving food boxes around and smiles as he sees me getting closer.

I stand on tiptoe to kiss him.

He turns to me and holds my hips gently in his hands. His head tips down and he joins me in the kiss.

For years and years I imagined what it might be like to kiss Robinson. I stood under the mistletoe at Christmas I don't know how many times, hoping he might accidentally step under there with me and then be required to kiss me. He never did, but that didn't stop me from dreaming about what it would feel like and taste like, to have his lips press against mine. I'm ashamed to think of how many times I practiced with my pillow.

Why I'm flashing back to memories of Robinson when I'm kissing a guy who played basketball for the Fighting Irish and has the body to show for it, I don't know. It's some evil trick karma is playing on me, making it impossible for me to enjoy good fortune when I finally get some in my life.

I pull away with a scowl.

He looks at me and blinks a few times before he speaks. "Wow. I wasn't expecting that."

"I know." I walk away and wave it off. "I'm sorry. I just... got carried away."

"I promise I can do better. You just took me by surprise."

He sounds so sincere, I have to smile. Looking up at him, I feel my face going a little red. He must think I'm insane. "Your kiss was perfect. There's nothing to improve on."

"Then why the horrible face after? Is it my breath?" He starts blowing into his palm and inhaling.

I reach out and punch him lightly in the arm. "Stop. It's not you. It's not your breath."

"Are you married?"

I pick up a samosa and sigh loudly. "I *will* throw this at your head."

He backs up and holds a plate up between us like a shield. "Knowing the way you throw a punch, I'm worried that'll go right into my eye. Put that Chinese star samosa down, young lady."

I laugh and drop it onto my plate. "Okay, fine. You're safe now. Come on. Serve yourself up and come into the family room. We can watch TV while we eat." My perfectly set table is going to stay that way, untouched. I'm not in the mood to be formal anymore. I've already ruined our night by bringing Robinson into it, and there's no way I'm sleeping with Jake tonight. For sure I'll be lying there comparing his body to the one I've imagine Robinson has without all his clothes on. I'm so completely pitiful, it's sickening.

Jake follows my lead and takes a seat on the couch, putting his now shoeless feet up on the coffee table. The two of us munch away on our samosas and kashmir rice. He gives me the best bites of his chicken tikka and I let him eat all the bits of dried fruit from my rice.

"I can't believe you like that stuff," I say, dropping more pieces onto his plate. "You probably like fruitcake too."

"I do," he says, eating a whole forkful of fluorescent, candied fruit bits. "Love it. Christmas is my favorite holiday just because of that."

I shake my head, pretending to be interested in the TV show. "I knew I'd discover your kryptonite eventually."

"My kryptonite?"

"Yeah. The chink in the armor. The thing that revealed you for who you truly are."

"I'm a fruitcake eater?"

"Yep." I look at sideways at him. "I knew you were too good to be true."

He pushes his rice around on his plate with his fork, his smile kind of sad. "Fruitcake isn't the only chink, trust me."

I stop chewing for a second and then narrow my eyes at him, intrigued. "Hmm, the man has secrets. Do tell."

He shakes his head. "I told you already… I'll share mine if you share yours."

"Fine." I lean forward and put my plate down on the coffee table. "I'm ready. Spill your guts."

"I'm still eating," he says, stabbing some chicken.

I take his plate away from him and put it next to mine. His fork is left dangling in the air in front of his open mouth.

"Last bite. Hurry up."

He slides the chicken off the fork and hands the utensil to me. "Bossy."

"Yup." I put his fork on his plate and then slide over to the far side of the couch, sitting with my legs folded up under me.

He slings his arm over the back of the couch and twists a little in my direction. "You go first."

I shake my head. "No. You go. I promise, though, I'll talk."

He sighs and then stares off into the distance, not really seeing me or my apartment. The lines in his face smooth out as he catches up with memories I already know are going to be difficult for him to dredge. I wait, giving him the time to gather his thoughts, wondering if I'm going to finally find out how a man as beautiful as he is can be so alone.

Chapter Eighteen

JAKE POKES HIS FINGER INTO his leg rhythmically as he talks, staring at the coffee table as the words first come reluctantly and then more quickly, as if he's relieved to get them off his chest.

"I was always in and out of trouble in school. Even when I played on the basketball team, I was messing around with drugs and alcohol. Pretty much everyone did, so it wasn't like I had a problem or anything. I still managed to keep up with the practices, and my grades weren't bad. But then I injured my shoulder and had to take the bench. The pain killers were pretty awesome, especially when mixed with the drinking."

He looks up at me and smiles sadly. "It was stupid, really. I thought I was invincible. But then one night I was messing around at a frat party and I fell out of a window and landed on a deck chair and really screwed my shoulder up."

"You fell out of a *window*?" I blink a few times, trying to imagine this calm and easygoing guy being that much of a party hound.

"Yeah. Like I said, I was being stupid. So I ended up needing surgery to fix a torn rotator cuff, which ended my basketball career."

"That sucks."

"Yeah. My scholarships disappeared, and I had to pay my own way. It wasn't easy, but I finished. Graduated."

"And that's it?" I was waiting for this big confession, but everything he's told me so far is easy to write off as youthful indiscretions. I've never fallen out of a window, but I have been to parties were people jumped out of them.

"Not exactly," he says, glancing at me and then staring at the table again.

"Uh-oh."

He smiles a little. "What?"

"Why do I think you told me the easy story first?"

He shrugs and looks at me. "Because I did?"

I reach out with a foot and nudge him with it before tucking it back under me. "Keep talking, buddy. I have dessert waiting for us."

"You may not want to share that dessert with me after I tell you."

I cringe. "Oh. Okay. I hope you didn't murder someone."

He shakes his head. "No, nothing like that. But bad enough that I won't hold it against you if you deny me the dessert and ask me to go."

He's serious, I can tell by the look on his face. I tuck my feet in tighter and wrap the throw blanket around my shoulders, trying to ward off the sudden chill in the room.

"Go ahead. I'll withhold judgment until you're done."

"Fair enough." He nods. Then he goes back to poking his leg as he stares at the TV. I'm sure he's not seeing the sitcom that's currently playing, though. His voice is nearly a monotone.

"I had a bad temper after my surgery. I was angry at myself, my friends, at the coach. Pretty much anyone was a target. And the pain was bad. I'm not saying that as an excuse for what I did, but it was. I was on about three different painkillers. The rehab was hard, harder than anything I'd ever had to do before, and I'd been playing sports my whole life."

I rub my shins, trying to get warm. The atmosphere in the room has gone so dark.

"I was dating this girl, Sophie, and I really liked her. I convinced myself I loved her and I was going to ask her to marry me, even though I really didn't have any prospects at the time."

He sighs heavily. "She started acting distant and then one night I went to a party and found her there with a guy from my team. I realized after a couple people said some things that it had been going on for a long time; I was the last to find out about it. And I thought the guy was my friend."

"That sucks."

"Yeah, well, it's still not an excuse. I took a baseball bat and destroyed his car. And then when he came outside and tried to stop me, I attacked him too."

"Oh, god." I can't even picture it. Jake is big, and I'm sure he could do some serious damage, especially with a bat, but his whole persona is so mild. I just can't imagine him getting that angry.

"Yeah. Put him in the hospital. Thank goodness the guys from the team were there to stop me, or I probably would've killed him."

"What happened after?"

He smiles, but there's no trace of happiness to it. "Oh, I got arrested. Got charged with aggravated battery. Got convicted and went to jail. I served almost a year before I was let out. Finished school, made amends, and started my life over..." He looks up at me, an apology in his eyes. "...As a convicted felon. It took me a long time to get my plumbing license and my bond so I could work on my own."

I want to cry for him, for the stupid mistakes he made as a kid. "That's a very sad story."

"Yeah, maybe." His mood changes for the better, his smile looking more heartfelt now. "I met a really cool guy in prison, though. He was there as the chaplain, but he was young and really energetic. He was a former gangbanger who turned his life around. He taught me about the importance of having a good attitude and accepting responsibility for my choices. He saved me. Saved my life, really."

I'm near tears, so happy for him. "That's so cool. Where is he now? Still at the prison?"

He shakes his head and stares at the table again. "No, he died. Cancer."

"Oh. Wow. That's awful." I move over closer to Jake on the couch, putting my hand on his arm. "I'm really sorry."

He looks up at me and smiles a little. "Thanks. He was a great guy. Helped a lot of people like me."

"Like you?" I search his face and see only a good person there.

"Lost boys. He saved lost boys."

"Seems like he did the whole world a favor," I say, hugging Jake.

He hugs me back. "Do I get to stay for dessert or is it time for me to go?"

I slap him lightly on the back of the head. "Don't piss me off." Pushing myself out of his arms, I stand and hold my hands out. "Come on. Let's go make some sundaes."

He takes my offer of help and pulls himself to his feet. Together we walk around the couch and head for the kitchen. I'm both happy that he's shared his past with me and scared. Because now I know I have to return the favor and open up my heart for his examination, and I'm not sure I can be as forthright with him about my mistakes as he's been with me about his.

Chapter Nineteen

I TAKE MY TIME BUILDING the perfect ice cream sundae, not because I love them so much but because I'm stalling for time. Jake is fully expecting me to confess all my secrets, but I'm not even sure what they are. They're not so much secrets as they're just sad commentaries on things that happened to me, and I hate the idea that my story doesn't have a happy ending like his does. Yes, he lost a friend, but he found himself. The lost boy is now the found boy, and as a result, his life is great. I'm still lost, and I have no idea how to find my way out of the darkness.

"So," he says, using his spoon to gather up a big puddle of chocolate syrup, "what's your deal? You a convicted felon too?"

I laugh, eating my cherry first. "No." I crunch away on it as he licks all the chocolate off his spoon. Maybe if it were another guy I'd consider it sexy, but when he does it, it's just silly. I really want to fling some whipped cream onto his face, but I don't. Whipped cream has way too many sexy connotations to be playing with it like that. Besides, he'll see right through it as the distraction technique that it is.

"I'm not a convicted felon, but I am a very screwed up individual."

"I find that hard to believe," he leans his butt on the counter and eats a big spoonful of ice cream as he waits for me to continue.

"Believe it." I keep eating, hoping he'll let me off the hook. I really don't want to talk about my family and what happened. It's making me sick to my stomach just thinking about it.

"I'm not going to force you to tell me," he says after a long period of silence.

"Really?" There's so much hope in my voice, it pisses me off. Since when did I become such a wiener, anyway?

He shrugs. "Nope. Not if you don't want to."

I shake my head, trying to push away the feelings of fear and inadequacy and shame. What happened, happened. I just need to figure out how to move on from it. Maybe talking to the guy who knew this priest will help me. Maybe he learned something from his friend the chaplain that could turn the light on for me.

I sigh and then just start talking. "My problems started when my sister-in-law was killed by a drunk driver when she was nine months pregnant."

He stops chewing his ice cream and slowly lowers his dish to the counter. Then he just stands there, still leaning on the counter, waiting for me to continue. I see nothing but concern in his expression, and it fuels me forward.

"She died, but the baby survived. We named her Cassiopeia because that's what Laura — my sister-in-law — asked us to do."

"So she survived for a little while?"

I shake my head. "No. She died in the ambulance, but she was always telling us she knew she was going to die young, and she was always saying stuff like, 'If I die, make sure you do this,' or whatever. We were instructed to name her child Cassiopeia and that's what we did. We call her Cassie for short."

"It's a beautiful name. And a beautiful gesture to grant her mother's wish like that."

"Yeah, well, my brother Jeremy —her husband— was destroyed. He flipped out. He never showed up to take Cassie home from the hospital."

"Wow."

"Yeah, wow. I did it, though. I took her home with me." I can still picture that moment, when I lifted her out of her plexiglass bassinet wrapped in the blanket I'd bought for Laura and given to her at her baby shower. I never imagined that I'd be the one taking her home from the hospital in it. Not in a million years would I have guessed that would happen.

"What about your brother? What did he do then?"

"He went off the deep end. Drugs, alcohol, you name it. If he could disappear from reality, he took the opportunity."

"And left you with the baby."

"Yes. But I preferred that to him trying to take care of her in the state he was in. He couldn't even care for himself let alone an infant."

"It couldn't have been easy for you. You were in mourning too."

I nod. He gets it. "Yes, I was. We all were. But Cassie had needs and those came first. For nine months I took care of her like she was my own."

"Don't you have other family? What about your parents?"

I shake my head. "Died years ago. I have another brother, James, but he's really busy with his medical practice."

"You're busy. Or I assume you were. Why were you the only one helping?"

I feel a little guilty taking all the credit for her care. James did step up to the plate eventually, when she was finally able to sleep through the night. "I wasn't the only one. James helped when he could. He took her some weekends after she was a few months old."

"You said you had her for nine months." He looks around the room. "I don't see any baby things here. How old is she now?"

"Almost one. She's been gone for a couple months now."

"Gone? Where?"

"With her father. He took her back."

Jake's expression goes dark. "How is that possible?"

I have the strangest urge to assure him it's all fine, that everything worked out. I'm not sure why, since my first instinct up until now has been to cry foul and complain how Cassie and I got screwed out of our life together. This internal conflict has me feeling decidedly uncomfortable.

"Jeremy got his shit together, I guess." I shrug, still not sure I believe it. "Stopped the drinking and the drugs, started going to meetings, met a *girl*." I try really really hard not to snarl at that last part, but I'm only partially successful.

"Ahhh, a girl." Jake folds his arms. "I take it you and this girl don't get along."

"Why would you say that?"

"I don't know. Just the way your face looked when you mentioned her."

I shrug. "She's nice enough. I met her before she met my brother. She's an artist and… polite."

He laughs. "Polite?"

I smile too. I knew it sounded stupid and petty when it left my mouth, but then it was too late to take it back. Damn. I really need to grow up. Jake's been to jail and back; I can hardly mope around and talk about how much my life sucks. At least I don't have a felony record following me around for the rest of my life.

"She's nice. I had some long conversations with her when we toured some museums together, and I liked her. But after my brother met her, just a few weeks later, supposedly his life was back on track and he was ready to be a dad again. I didn't buy it."

"And now? How are they doing?"

I want to kick the wall in. "They're doing fine, I guess."

"You guess? Don't you know?"

My face burns with shame. "No. I haven't seen them in a long time. Since they got married, not long after they took Cassie."

Jake pushes himself off the counter and comes over to wrap his arms around me. I stand there accepting his embrace but not returning the gesture.

He rests his chin lightly on my head. "Sounds like you've had to deal with some pretty serious losses over the last year."

I nod, unable to speak without crying, hugging my ice cream dish to my chest.

"I can see why you feel like everything's out to get you."

I slide my arms and ice cream bowl around his waist to rest at his lower back. The smell of his shirt and warmth eases the pain in my heart. I slip the bowl onto the counter next to his.

"What I can't figure out is why you bought that house in the middle of all of it. Are you a glutton for punishment or what?"

I laugh, surprised that he's able to make me smile when I should be crying. "Shut up."

He pulls back so he can look at me. "You're a brave girl. And I don't blame you one bit for being pissed at the world."

"Thank you." I release one of my arms from his waist to wipe under my eyes. They were just about to leak a tear or two.

"Can I share with you the things I learned from Father Carlos?"

I shrug. "I guess."

"I promise I won't preach."

"Good. Because preachers get a one-way ticket out the front door."

He pulls back from me and takes me by the hand. "Come sit with me on the couch. I'll share my last secret with you before I go."

I follow behind, wondering if he'll really leave when it's all over or ask me if he can stay the night. I'm not sure what I'll say if he does.

Chapter Twenty

JAKE AND I SIT ON the couch and share a glass of wine between us. We're positioned closer to one another than we were before, and there's a sense of having made it through hard times between us. It's totally crazy, of course, since he's my plumber and I still hardly know him. But still, I like the sense of comfort he brings by being near. I'm not going to fight the things that feel good tonight; it's been too long since I've felt truly happy, and here next to him, I'm almost there.

"Carlos was this guy who walked around covered in tattoos but with a light kind of shining out from inside him." Jake smiles. "It was crazy, but everyone saw it. Even the hardcore criminals who were never going to get out of there. When Carlos talked, everyone listened. Not everyone internalized what he said, of course, but they at least let him speak."

"Do you mean like a sermon?"

Jake shakes his head. "No. He never preached. That's what I liked about him. He never quoted a bible verse or anything that I ever noticed. He never said anything about Jesus or whatever.

He just lived like Jesus would have, I guess you could say. I know a lot of religious people say, 'What would Jesus do?' but I say, 'What would Carlos do?' and I always end up on the right path if I try to follow his example."

"Huh." I'm non-comittal because I can't imagine a person being that good in this day and age. We all have our Kryptonite, and I'm sure Carlos wasn't an exception. But still, if he had this much of an impact on Jake's life, I'm interested in hearing what he had to say.

"Carlos talked a lot about choices. About how everything we do and see in our lives is a matter of choice." Jake looks at me, handing me the glass of wine for my turn at sipping. "We're all presented with situations every day where we have to make a choice. We can react one way or another. We choose which way we end up reacting, for better or for worse."

I shake my head. "Sometimes people make the choice for you."

"No, not really. Things happen, sure, but you make the choice how it affects you, if you think about it."

I shake my head. "Not in my case."

"Yes, in your case. In everyone's case."

He's starting to piss me off. Clearly, he wasn't paying attention to my story earlier. "Someone took my child from me. You're saying I had a choice in that?"

He takes the wine glass from me and puts it on the table. "As I see it, Cassie was returned to her father. Is that right? From a legal perspective, I mean."

I want to push him away from me, but I'm an adult and I can handle a difficult conversation without resorting to violence, so I don't. But I do lean a little away from him. His closeness isn't quite as appealing anymore.

"Maybe."

"Okay, so of course it hurt your feelings and broke your heart when it happened. You probably felt like people let you down. People you cared about."

He's perceptive, I'll give him that. I didn't even tell him about the part Robinson played in the whole thing.

"Of course," I say, slightly mollified.

"You had a choice about how to react to that. You could have focused entirely on the immediate emotional responses, like heartache and distrust and disappointment... or you could have focused on other things."

"Other things? Are you kidding me? Apparently you've never lost a child." So much for enlightenment. I'm starting to think this guy Carlos was a simple spin doctor, nothing more.

"Yes, other things. Like how joyful it must have been for her father to feel like he could care for his child, finally — the child he created with his wife who was taken from him much too early, much too young."

Guilt stabs me right in the heart. I grit my teeth together to keep from saying anything rude.

"Like how good it will be for Cassie when she's old enough to understand that she's with her father, the man who loved her mother, who can share his love for her mother with her as she grows older."

Tears start to build. I'm really starting to dislike Jake and his stupid philosophies on life.

"And like how it will be for you, to be able to continue with your life as it was, looking for someone to share your life with and maybe have children with if that's what you want to do. Plus, you'll have a much closer relationship with Cassie you wouldn't have had otherwise..."

I stand, because I can't hear any more of this garbage. "Stop. Just stop."

"I'm sorry." He looks sad. "Am I upsetting you? I didn't mean to."

I pinch the bridge of my nose and close my eyes, trying to get a handle on my runaway emotions and the headache blossoming from somewhere deep in my skull. I know he doesn't mean to be destroying me with every single word; he's just trying to help. I can't hate him for that, but I also can't be around him right now. He's just another person making excuses for my brothers and Robinson, telling me I need to get over everything and suck it up.

"It's fine. I have a headache. It kind of just snuck up on me. Do you mind?" I turn to face the door.

"You sure you don't want me to stay and make you some tea or anything?"

I shake my head, dropping my hands and rubbing them on my jeans. "No, that's all right. I'm just going to go to bed, I think."

Jake follows me around the couch and takes my hand as I try to walk away.

"Hey. I'm sorry."

I shrug, pulling my hand away. "No, it's not a problem. Don't apologize. I appreciate you sharing your stuff with me."

"You weren't ready to hear it, though."

"Ready?" As if there's a timeframe for acting like stuff didn't happen the way it did. I want to laugh, but I realize he means well, so I won't mock his personal philosophies.

"Ready to deal with the issue." He elaborates. "Ready to face the music."

My temper's starting to flare, so I give him the best smile I can manage and walk to the door. "See you on the job," I say as cheerily as possible. "Thanks so much for dinner. Again."

"No problem. Anytime. Maybe you'd like to throw a frisbee in the park sometime."

I can't laugh at his joke; I'm liable to start bawling.

He pauses at the door like he's contemplating asking for a goodbye kiss, and I get ready to slap him across the face for even asking, but both potential futures are stopped in their tracks when a buzzer sounds off just next to my face.

I jump, my eyes bugging out of my head. *What the...?*

When my brain connects the dots and realizes that horrible sound exacerbating my headache is someone calling me from downstairs, I step over and press the button on the intercom, wondering who in the hell is trying to buzz in after midnight.

"Who's there?" I ask.

"It's me." The voice says, the words slurred. "It's Robinson."

I let out a long sigh and rest my head on the wall next to the intercom box.

Jake doesn't say a word.

A moment later, I lift my head, press the button, and speak. "Stay there. I'm coming down."

Chapter Twenty-One

THE ELEVATOR RIDE TO THE ground floor of my building will go down in history as one of the most awkward moments of my life. Jake has no place asking me who the man buzzing me in the middle of the night is, but I know he's curious as hell. He keeps clearing his throat and looking at me and then the floor and the ceiling. I keep my eyes glued to the doors, praying Robinson will go away before I get there. What's Jake going to say? I didn't even tell Jake about him. Will he think I hid that detail on purpose? Did I?

Why did Robinson have to show up now? And why does it feel like he saved me from an uncomfortable situation? For the first time in months, a sliver of gratitude toward him sneaks in, and that just pisses me off more. I shouldn't be looking at Robinson as my hero. Jake was just being a nice guy, trying to help me find a solution the way he did in his own life. It's not his fault that it won't work for me. I'm sure a lot of people would appreciate his efforts.

God, my life is so completely screwed up. If gravity reversed and I suddenly had to start walking on the ceiling, I wouldn't be surprised. Par for the course at this point.

Of course my prayers for Robinson to disappear aren't answered. No such luck. I can see his dark figure through the ice-frosted glass of the front doors as I step out of the elevator.

"I feel kind of strange about leaving you here with that guy," Jake says, walking next to me. "Do you know him well?" We're almost to the front doors when he stops and waits for my answer.

"Yes," I say, feeling utterly defeated. Karma hates me. This I now know as a fact. "He's our family attorney."

Jake mulls that over for a few seconds before responding. "You mean the same lawyer who handled all the business with Cassie?"

"Bingo," I say with false cheer. "Five points for guessing correctly."

He looks out the window at Robinson and then at me. "And he's visiting you at your place in the middle of the night? Drunk?"

His implication that Robinson and I are in a relationship is impossible to miss. I sigh loudly, and as the air leaves my lungs, literally collapse in on myself. My shoulders slump and my backbone turns to jelly. I wish I could just say it out loud, the thing that eats away at my heart on a daily basis: the man who I've loved for more than half my life, the same man who helped take my child away from me, is the one standing out there beyond the glass doors. But I can't say that. Of course I can't. I have to be a grown up and say what everyone would expect of me.

"He's an old family friend. I've known him since I was a kid." Rejection, rejection, rejection. Jake will never know the truth: that I was in love with Robinson for over fifteen years and he never even looked at me twice before destroying my life.

"I take it he's an old boyfriend?"

My head jerks up and I'm instantly mad over even the suggestion that there was ever anything between Robinson and me. "What? Me? Us? No? Whatever gave you that idea?" I don't even know why I wanted that for so long anymore. I must have been deaf, dumb, and blind to moon over him for so long.

Jake looks at me and then Robinson again. His head drops and he shoves his hands in his pockets. "No reason. Listen, I'd better get going. That guy's probably freezing out there."

The smoke from Robinson's breath lingers all around him, and he's got the Manhattan hunchback syndrome going, his body folding over on itself as he tries to stay warm.

"So what?" I say, feeling callously bitchy. "He can freeze his butt off out there for all I care."

Jake gives me a bittersweet smile. "Yeah. Right." He turns and heads for the door.

"What's that supposed to mean?" I ask, pissed all over again. What's he suggesting? That I do care about Robinson? Because I don't. I seriously don't.

"Nothing. See you on the job site." He walks outside and holds the door open for a few seconds, getting Robinson's attention.

Robinson turns his head as he grabs the door before it shuts, watching Jake walk out to the curb and hail a passing cab.

"Who's that guy?" Robinson asks as he walks inside the lobby, still distracted by my visitor. I watch as Jake folds his tall frame into the back of the cab. He doesn't even look over to say good-bye, but I can't find it in me to care very much. *Boomp, boomp, boomp, another one bites the dust.*

"None of your business." I turn my attention to Robinson and fold my arms, trying to stay warm in the suddenly cold foyer. "What are you doing here so late?"

Robinson pops up and down on his toes, his arms stiff at his sides. "I don't know. I was in the neighborhood. Thought I'd drop by to see how you're doing."

I stare at him, wishing I could read his mind. He stares back at me, his teeth chattering. It's on the tip of my tongue to send him away, to put him back out there into the freezing cold night... but I don't. Of course I don't. The words won't come out of my mouth, much as I want them to, and I can smell the liquor on his breath. Imagining him falling down and passing out on the side-walk makes me worry for him. Instead of kicking him out to the street where he belongs, I turn back toward the elevator and press the call button.

"Can I come up?" he asks.

"Can I stop you?"

"I'd rather you didn't."

I shake my head, disgusted with us both. "Just shut up and get in the elevator." The doors open and I step inside, waiting until Robinson is inside before I press the button for my floor.

Chapter Twenty-Two

S O, YOU HAD A DATE over," Robinson says as we ride the
elevator up to my floor.

"That's none of your business, I already told you." I can't look
at him. I stare at the buttons instead. It seems like the elevator is
going in slow motion.

"He that plumber guy?"

I glare at him. "I'm pretty sure none of your business means
you have no right to try and identify him."

"I'm just being friendly." He tries to smile at me, but it slips
when he loses his balance. It's then that I realize how drunk he
really is.

"No, you're just being nosy. Who really sent you here? Was
it James?"

"No." He laughs and then starts talking in kind of a singsong
voice. "In fact, your brother James is being very protective of you
if you really want to know."

The elevator doors slide open with a ding. I step out and turn
around, holding them open as I study Robinson's face. "What's

that supposed to mean?" Generally speaking, my brother James is kind of his own entity. He knows I'm his sister and everything, but I wouldn't categorize him as overly interested in my life. We used to get together for dinner once in a while, but that's the extent of our adult sibling relationship. There's kind of a big age gap between us.

Robinson smiles lazily as he walks up to me, stopping on the edge of the elevator. "He warned me away. Big scary big brother." He wiggles his fingers at his shoulders like some kind of zombie ghoul.

I shake my head and let my hand fall away from the doors. I don't care if he gets smooshed between them anymore. Walking over to my door, I stop just in front of it, not looking to see if he's behind me. He can sleep in the elevator for all I care. At least then I won't have to worry about him freezing to death out in an alley somewhere.

He follows me with shuffling feet and leans on the wall as I open the door. I'm pretty sure he's using the hallway for support because he'd fall over if he tried to stand entirely on his own power.

"How much did you drink, anyway?" I ask, shutting the door behind him when he abandons the foyer for the couch. He falls down onto it, his overcoat bunching up around him. His hands are stuck in the pockets, and I watch with amusement as he tries to free them, but then gives up. He slumps down in the cushions and stares at the blank TV screen.

"I don't know. A couple."

"I hope you're not driving."

"Nah. Got a cab."

"Who were you with?" I walk into the kitchen and put on a pot of coffee. I have a feeling Rob's going to need a couple cups of it before he leaves. Hopefully he won't piss me off too much and force me to kick him out before I get the caffeine into his system.

"Nobody. Just me. All alone in a bar. Sad huh?" He tips his head back over the couch to look at me. His eyes close and then he winces, picking his head back up. I suspect room-spins are at the root of his movements.

After grabbing a bottle of water from the fridge and two ibuprofen pills from the cabinet, I join him in the living room. "Here. Take these."

He opens his eyes and blinks a few times deliberately, trying to reorient himself. "What's that?" He eyes my offerings with suspicion.

"Drugs. I'm roofying you."

He grins and nearly gives me a heart attack with it. Dammit, he can be so cute sometimes.

"Sweet. You're finally coming around." He grabs the pills and throws them into his mouth and then takes the water, talking around the ibuprofen on his tongue. "Sure took you long enough."

I roll my eyes and stand, making sure to kick him as I walk by.

"Ow! Was that deliberate?" He bends over and rubs his shin as I go into the kitchen. Then he swigs the water.

"No less than what you deserve."

He sighs loud enough for me to hear. "You're right. Go ahead and grab a frying pan while you're in there. Bash me in a head a few times. I can take it."

I pour him a cup of coffee and put in the two spoons of sugar I know he likes. My gaze strays over to the cupboard with the pots and pans, but I abandon the flicker of a thought as soon as it arrives. I don't want to give Rob a head injury; I just want him to leave me alone. He'll probably see a bap upside the head with a skillet as an invitation to stay the night.

I go back into the living room with the cup of coffee in hand. "Here," I say, putting it down on the coffee table, "drink this." I sit down a couple cushions over from him.

"Mmmm, hemlock tea. My favorite." He takes the mug and then almost drops it in his haste to put it back down on the coffee table. "Oo-ah! That was hot." He blows on his fingers.

I lift a brow at him. "That's why they have handles."

"They?" he asks, his expression classic confused.

"Coffee mugs." It crosses my mind that this must be what it feels like to babysit someone with a head injury.

"Oh, yeah." He looks at the mug and then at me. "Did you just make that for me?"

"Yes."

"Did you put two sugars in it?"

"I did."

His face quivers and then crumples, and before I realize what he's up to, he falls sideways and grabs me in a hug, trapping my arms at my sides. "Thank you so much!" he sobs.

I sit there stunned, completely clueless. "Uhhh, okay. You're welcome, I guess."

"You made me coffee." He's actually crying. "With two sugars."

"Yeesss, I did. Yay me?"

He releases me from his imprisoning hug, but slides his cold hands down to grip mine. He's staring into my eyes, close enough that I can smell his breath. It might be possible to actually light his breath on fire, had I a candle nearby. Phew. He must have bought a bottle.

"You still care about me," he says, the sound of relief in his voice.

I roll my eyes and push him away. "Get over yourself, Rob."

"And you called me Rob!" He traps me in another hug, his face pressed sideways against my breasts.

Try as I might, I can't pry him off me. After attempting my release for a few seconds, I give up and just wait for his chick moment to be over.

He mumbles into my arm. "I thought you hated me. That you were never going to talk to me again. But you made me coffee with sugar and you called me Rob. Now I know all's not lost."

Maybe I should be charmed, but instead, he's making me angry with his stupid declarations. Does he really think it's all that easy? That he can show up drunk, I'll feel sorry for him and try to sober him up for the ride home, and that somehow this means I love him again?

Just thinking the word *love* in my head makes me furious.

"Get off me!" I yell shoving on his shoulder.

He sits back and is once again confused. "What's wrong?"

I shake my head, glaring at him. "You're drunk and you stink. I don't want you here, so I'm sobering you up enough to put you in a cab. Don't read anything more into it than it is."

His hand lifts and rests on his chest. "Ow. That hurt."

"Shut up."

"No, I mean it." He winces. "Fuck, that hurts." He pushes his thumb into his chest and twists it around.

"Good."

He reaches for the coffee, but stops midway, grabbing his chest with his other hand. "Ow, mother fu..." He bends over at the waist until his chest is lying on his legs.

"Are you okay?" I'm starting to worry that he's not messing around.

"It burns," he grunts out.

I jump off the couch and stand in front of him on the opposite side of the table, my mind dancing at the edge of panic. "Rob! Seriously! Cut it out!"

His voice comes out as a moaning growl. "I'm not messing around."

"Oh my god, oh my god, oh my god! What are you *doing*?! You can't have a heart attack here!"

He slides from the couch to the floor and acts like he's going to crawl to the door. "Okay," he moans. "I'll do it outside."

"No!" I run over to block him and grab my phone from the front table, hitting the speed dial for my brother James.

He picks up on the fifth ring, saving me from the panic attack his voicemail would have given me.

"James!" I scream before he can even speak.

"No, it's me Leah. What's wrong? Is this Jana?"

"Get James! Get James! I need to talk to him right now!" I'm crying. I'm not even sure when I started. Was it when Rob started crawling toward the door or when he collapsed on the floor on top of his own arms?

I run over and drop to my knees on the floor next to him. "Rob! Are you okay?!"

"Jana, what's wrong?" James's steady, patient voice is in my ear. It takes me a second to realize it's because I have the phone there.

"Rob is here, and I think he's having a heart attack."

"Here where?"

"My apartment."

"What's he …? Never mind. Call 9-1-1. I'll meet you at the hospital. Text me which one. Tell them you're his wife."

"His wife?"

"Just do it, Jana!"

"Okay!" I cry out. "You don't have to yell at me!"

"I'm sorry. Call 9-1-1. Now." He hangs up and leaves me staring at my phone.

Chapter Twenty-Three

I DIAL 9-1-1, all the while leaning over Rob, trying to see if he's still breathing. As soon as my face is close enough to his mouth, though, I know he's alive. That breath of his … damn. This better not be just heartburn. I'll kill him for making me worry so much.

All I can think about is Laura's shiny, black casket, how dark and final it felt. The end of everything. And now Robinson is lying on my floor, breathing but no longer making jokes and not crying anymore about the coffee I made him with two sugars.

"9-1-1, what's your emergency?"

My words come out in a tumble. "I think my friend… I mean my husband is having a heart attack."

"What's your address?"

I rattle off the information and push Rob over onto his back. His eyelids flutter but don't open. When he moans, a rush of relief pours into me from somewhere unknown. I lean down and hug him as best I can while holding the phone to my ear.

"Is he breathing?" the operator asks.

"Yes."

"Is he conscious?"

"No. Maybe. I can't tell." I poke his cheek a few times and he winces. "Maybe a little if I poke him."

"Best not to poke him, ma'am."

I yank my hand away. How'd she know I was just about to do it again? "Oh. Okay. No more poking."

"No more poking," Rob whispers. Then he smiles.

I'm torn between slapping him and crying. Instead, I opt for basic communication. Maybe if I keep him talking, he'll be okay and he won't die and leave me totally alone.

"Rob. Rob!" I lean down near his face and turn up the volume to maximum. *"ROB!"*

His eyes fly open and then roll around in his head. They're bloodshot and glassy. "What? Damn. Was that really loud or are my eardrums fucked up from the whiskey?"

Tears trickle down my cheeks. "I swear to God, Rob… if you're not having a heart attack, I'm going to kill you." I punch him in the arm so he knows I mean it.

"You love me," he says, his eyes closing as his grin widens.

I have to turn away so he won't see my tears turn into silent sobs. *Please, God, don't take him from me. Don't take him from us, I mean.* I think about how devastated James would be to lose his best friend. We can't lose someone again. Not this soon. Not Rob.

"Ma'am, the paramedics are on their way. Is there a door code they should know or do you have a doorman?"

I take a big breath to steady myself so I can at least talk. "I'll buzz them up when they come. I'm waiting right by the door." I use the heel of my free hand to wipe the wetness from my cheeks. My throat is aching with unshed tears, but I'm determined to hold it together. For Rob. I don't want him to think the situation is hopeless. *Please, God, don't let it be hopeless.*

"Good enough. How old is your husband?"

"Thirty seven."

"Approximate weight?"

"One ninety-five? Two hundred? Something like that."

"Health problems?"

"None that I know of."

"No history of heart problems?"

"No." Other than breaking them, no.

"So you said this is your husband?"

"Yes."

"How long have you been married?"

I blink a few times, trying to figure out why that matters. "Is that relevant to him having a heart attack?"

The operator laughs. "No, I was just being friendly. I have the information I need. I have to stay on the line with you until the unit arrives."

"Oh. Okay."

"So? How long have you been married?"

"We're newlyweds." The answer pops out of my head that way because I'm afraid she'll start quizzing me on what year we tied the knot, and I can't do math very well under pressure. This feels like a test, and I can picture the woman hanging up on me when she finds out Rob really isn't my husband. Oh, you lied? Sorry. I'm canceling your ambulance.

I reach out and pet his face, worried because it's gone slack again.

"Being a newlywed can be stressful," the oh-so-helpful operator says. I get the feeling she's blaming this heart attack on me. I rest my hand on Rob's chest just to be sure I can still feel a beat beneath his shirt. Sure enough, it's there. And I'm no doctor, but it seems nice and steady. I want to cry with relief, but I don't. I have to be strong for Rob.

"Sure," I say. "But being single can be stressful too."

"No doubt."

Rob's hand slides up and takes mine off his chest. Then to my surprise, he lifts it to his lips and kisses it.

"Don't ever leave me again," he says softly.

I'm too stunned to claim my hand back.

"You broke my heart, you know," he continues.

I try to pull my hand away, but his grip tightens and he kisses my fingers again. "It was horrible. Don't ever do that to me again." His words trail off and he goes silent again.

"Did you guys have a fight?" the woman asks.

I pull the phone away from my head and stare at it. She's definitely blaming me for this call.

I put the phone back to my head. "No, we didn't have a fight."

"He said you broke his heart."

My temper starts to rise again. "Excuse me, but is that any of your business? My god, I didn't call the relationship hotline instead of 9-1-1, did I?"

"No ma'am, you didn't. And I apologize. I'm just trying to be friendly."

I want to stay mad, but now I feel bad that I was so rude. "If you must know, *he* broke *my* heart."

Robinson's grip on my hand tightens. Then his other hand comes up to join the first and he pushes my palm into his chest.

I hate that he looks like he's been laid to rest in a coffin with his hands like that. I put the phone down so I can grab his chin. I shake his head back and forth. "Rob. Rob! Wake up."

He blinks his eyes a few times and then opens them fully. He tries to focus on me, but he's too drunk or too sick. It's impossible to tell. "Hi," he says, like he just woke up after spending the night on my floor.

"Are you okay?" I ask, the tears welling up again. My hand pats the floor for the phone. When I find it, I put it to my ear again. Hopefully I haven't missed anything important from Dear Abby-911-Operator on the other end of the line.

"My chest hurts," he says, pouting a little.

I lean down and kiss him on the forehead. "The ambulance is on the way."

"Ambulance? You called an ambulance?"

I nod, breathing through my nose to try and control my emotions. My entire face trembles with the effort. I hate seeing him look so vulnerable. It scares me, reminding me that life is so tenuous, so temporary. You never know when it'll be your time to go. Laura was right about that, like she was about a lot of things.

Time passes as I stare at Rob. I re-memorize all the features of his face, ever last wrinkle, every last eyelash. He's so beautiful it makes my heart ache. I stroke his forehead, his cheeks, his hair, trying to share my energy with him to keep him alive until someone is here to help.

Sometime later, Dear Abby-911-Operator comes back on the line. "Ma'am, the ambulance has arrived. Are you in a position to buzz them in?"

"Yes." I jump to my feet, pulling my hand from Rob's grip. I get to the door just as the buzzer's going off. Pressing the button, I lean toward the speaker. "Come on up. I have the door open for you. Twenty-fifth floor."

The sounds of traffic and banging come over the speaker. "On our way," a man says. And then I really start crying. *Please God, don't take him from me.*

Chapter Twenty-Four

THEY WON'T LET ME RIDE in the ambulance, no matter how much I bitch and scream about being Rob's wife. Thankfully, I find a cab willing to follow behind the emergency vehicle and keep up behind the thing as it speeds through the city. We swerve into the hospital's emergency entrance right behind it. I throw some money at the driver and run out, leaving him to argue with the security guards telling him to get lost.

A nurse stops me just inside the door, telling me I need to follow her to her desk to fill out paperwork. It's just a trick, though. I do as she asks, but she puts me in a waiting room so I can *wait* to fill out paperwork.

I whip my phone out and call James.

"Where are you?" he says without preamble.

"Bellevue."

"I'll be there in ten."

"They're making me wait to fill out paperwork." I drop my voice so no one nearby will hear me. "There's like fifteen other people in here. She says I can't see Rob until he's been seen by a doctor."

"Did you tell them you're his wife?"

"Yes."

"Give someone there the phone. Whoever's in charge."

I look around in fear. Will I start a riot getting preferential treatment? I stand a second later, not caring what anyone thinks. I need to make sure Rob's okay. I need to tell him it's okay. That what he did... I can forgive him for it. I can walk away and stop letting it tear me apart. Jake's earlier words come back to me and make me feel guilty all over again. He was just trying to help me and I basically kicked him out. He was right. He was completely right. I have a choice about how I'm handling this and I need to fix my mistakes.

I find the nurse who told me to sit down and smile at her, holding out my phone. "Hi there. I'm sorry to bother you, but ..."

"I told you to have a seat." She narrows her eyes at me.

"I know, but..."

"And now you're standing here holding a phone out at me."

"I know, but..."

"There are eleven people ahead of you, and I'm busy. Please go sit down." She glares at me over the top of her reading glasses.

If someone were sitting there being helped, I might have been more intimidated by her attitude. But she's eating a sandwich and texting someone. I can see the beginning of a message on her screen and her thumb hovering over the buttons.

I put the phone to my ear and talk to my brother a little louder than normal. "Did you get that, *Doctor* Oliver?"

Her head comes up and her expression changes just the slightest bit. "You have your physician on the line?"

"Actually, I have my brother on the line. James Oliver. Do you know him?"

She smiles and reaches for the phone. "Of course I know James. Everyone knows James." She takes my cell and pinches it between her face and her shoulder as she grabs a clipboard and starts attaching papers to it from a stack in some paper trays on her desk. "Doctor O! How are you? It's Sally down here in the ER."

She nods and uh-huhs, and umm-hmmm a few times and then she smiles. "Okay. I'll tell her. See you soon. Don't forget to drop by and say hi." She hangs up the call and hands the phone back to me, her face completely transformed by her smile. "Doctor Oliver said to let you go on in. If you'll step around to that door over there, I'll show you to your husband's bed."

I can't believe it was that easy. I feel guilty my connections are getting me into the inner sanctum but not guilty enough to say no thanks to her invitation. Thankfully, the door she points me to isn't near the other people waiting to fill out their paperwork.

When I get to the double doors the nurse gestured to, I'm tempted to hold them open and yell, 'Run everyone! Find your loved ones while you can!' But of course I don't. I do what I'm told and find myself led around a very busy-looking nurse's station to a curtained-off cubicle that has a bed and my brother's former college roommate lying in it.

His eyes are closed and there are wires coming out from under the blanket covering him. His complexion looks horrible, more gray than anything else.

"Oh my god," I whisper, my hand going to my mouth. "What did I do?"

Rob's eyes open and he looks right at me, but I see no recognition there. Then, slowly he smiles and his skin doesn't look quite so terrible. "Hey there."

"Hey." I walk closer, stopping at the side of his bed. "How are you feeling?"

"I've felt better." He looks me up and down. "What's a nice girl like you doing in a place like this?"

"Shut up or I'll pinch off your air hose." I point to the tube going into his nose, connected to a plug on the wall.

"Nice." He smiles and nods. "I'm glad to see my near-death experience hasn't changed your opinion of me."

Tears spring to my eyes and I reach my hand out.

He cringes, waiting for me to smack him, but instead I wipe the hair from his eyes.

His gaze follows my fingers and then moves to my face. When he begins to talk, his voice catches, so he clears his throat and starts over. "So, did you have a hard time getting past the guards out front?"

"Not once I got the nurse on the phone with James I didn't."

"You called James?" He looks off to the side. "Dammit."

I stop playing with his hair and rest my hand on his arm. "Why dammit?"

He sighs. "No reason in particular."

Just then the curtain twitches to the side and James himself walks in. He's followed by a younger guy in a white coat holding a clipboard. I get the distinct impression he's an intern or resident or something. I remember my brother going through the rigorous medical training, and he looked just like this guy does: young, a little scared, and like he hasn't slept in a week.

"Robinson," he says, coming over to stand next to me.

Relief finally starts flowing when my brother's arm goes around me and he squeezes me up against him. "How are you feeling?"

"I'm fine," Rob and I say at the same time.

James glares at Rob. "I wasn't talking to you."

Rob waves his hand weakly up from the bed. "My bad. Sorry. Thought you were talking to the guy who had a heart attack."

James looks over at the stranger in the cubicle. "Tell him your diagnosis, would you? So we can stop listening to him whine."

The intern clears his throat. "Based on the blood test we had analyzed in the lab, it doesn't appear as if you had any cardiac event."

Rob frowns. "But my chest ... the pain was terrible."

James turns to the intern again. The young guy pushes his glasses up and continues. "Based on your symptoms and the presence of a higher than normal blood alcohol level, my professional opinion is that you're suffering from a peptic ulcer."

"That sounds bad," Rob says in hushed tones.

"It's not," James says. "Stop drinking, stop smoking, and take some antibiotics. You'll be fine."

Everyone looks at James, I'm sure all of us thinking the same thing: what in the heck happened to his bedside manner?

"Does this mean I can leave?" Rob asks.

All three of us answer at the exact same time. "No!"

I look at the doctors. "You can't let him leave. He's sick! He practically died on my living room floor."

"I wasn't dying," Rob says, sounding embarrassed.

"My question is, what was he doing on your living room floor?" James asks. He glares first at Rob and then at me.

The intern slowly backs out of the room, letting the curtain fall into place after he's clear of it.

"Why are you mad at me?" I ask, stunned at his attitude. "I didn't do anything wrong?"

"Are you sure about that?" he asks.

My jaw drops open. I'm so frigging confused, I don't know what to say.

"It's not her fault, it's mine." Rob sighs. "I went over there after I left the bar. She felt bad for me. She offered me a cup of coffee to sober me up."

James turns his attention to Rob. "I told you to stay away from her."

I slap James on the arm with the back of my hand. "Hey! Who says you get to decide what Rob does?"

James glares at me for a second before going back to staring Rob down. "Rob can do whatever the hell he wants, just not with my sister."

The entire ER goes silent, except for the beeping of machines and hissing of air hoses.

"Oh my god," I whisper, pinching him. "Could you be any louder?" My face is burning with embarrassment. I can't even look at Rob.

"I know you told me to leave her alone, but I couldn't. I had to get her to just listen to me."

"I told you before, and now I'm going to tell you again with Jana here listening … Jana doesn't want to hear what you have to say. She wants you to leave her alone, and I want you to do the same. You did what you had to do, and we appreciate it, but now you just need to give us some space."

I sneak a glance at Rob and my heart nearly breaks at the pain I see there. But he presses his lips together and nods. "No problem."

"Rob…" I reach out to him, but James takes me by the arm and pulls me back. Rob just keeps staring at James, giving me the impression that I don't even exist anymore.

"Leave him be," James says, pulling me out of the curtained cubicle. We're standing in the aisle next to the nurse's station where everyone's acting like they didn't just hear everything that was said.

"Get off me," I hiss, yanking my arm out of his grasp.

"Listen," James says, his voice low but angry. "You need to stop leading him on."

"What?!" I cannot believe he just said that.

"Stop calling him, stop trying to see him, stop thinking about him that way."

"*What*?!" I thought my face was red before, but it can't have been even close to what it is now. I feel like I'm about to spontaneously combust. What I want to do is scream at my brother at the top of my lungs and tell him that he's not the boss of me and that he has this whole situation very, very wrong. But I can't, because there's an audience watching and I can't trust myself to stay reasonably calm. I'm liable to start throwing stethoscopes and computers around the room if I get started telling James what I think about him trying to tell me what to do with my life.

I settle for one statement before making my exit. Leaning in, I poke him in the center of the chest, and growl my words out. "You don't get to decide what I do with my life, so back the fuck off."

I spin around and walk to the nearest door, angry when I open it and find a bunch of blankets stacked up inside a closet. I leave that door open and continue down the hall, opening door after door until I finally get to a large set of double ones that open when someone walks up on the other side.

Fifteen minutes later, I finally find my way out to the street and take a cab home. It's four in the morning before I can finally stop fuming enough to go to bed. Just before I climb between the sheets, I send off a text. I think it's the magic trick that helps my brain to finally stop racing and relax.

Hi, Rob. It's me. We need to talk. Text me to tell me where and when, and I'll be there.

Chapter Twenty-Five

KEEPING BUSY WITH HOME RENOVATIONS isn't keeping my mind occupied enough. I check my phone all day long and into the night, waiting for a response from Rob, but nothing comes. Not the next day, or the next, or the next week even. Now I feel like I'm the one having a heart attack. A slow, painful ache settles deep into my chest and won't go away, no matter what I do. Leah's assurances that he's fine and that his ulcer is under control are nice to have, but they do nothing for the other issue between us. Not that there's an *Us* or anything, thanks to my stupid brother.

Rob has obviously decided to cut me off. I guess James is the boss of him. The only one who cares if I'm still alive is Leah, but I've put off her invitations to lunch and dinner every time she calls. I just can't work up the energy to be social. My life feels like it's in limbo right now, and limbo is a very lonely place.

I hate James. I hate having two older brothers. All they do is screw things up and break me into pieces. I feel bad for my subcontractors. Before I was letting little things slide, like when the grout between the bathroom tiles wasn't exactly the color I wanted or when the gutters around the new roof were a little slanted. But not anymore. I'm paying top dollar for this work, and I expect to get top-dollar quality out of it, dammit. The only guy who is getting a break from me is Jake the plumber, but he's the only one who doesn't need a break. He's more demanding of his work than I am.

"It's fine," I say for the third time, staring at the plumbing fixture in the bathroom with him.

"I don't like it," he responds. It's not in keeping with the style in here."

"I can get another one later. Just leave it like this."

"No. I'll get a new one tonight on my way home. It'll be installed no later than Friday."

It's been two weeks since our date, and I was expecting to have an awful time working with him so closely after, but he's been acting like it's no big deal. Making it easier is probably the fact that he hasn't been here as much the last few days, what with his part of the job winding down. I'll be a little sad to see him go, actually. Not only is he way cuter than any of the other subs running around, showing their hairy butt cracks off whenever they bend over, but he has a good heart; every time I look at him I think about what he said, about his pastor friend Carlos and what he taught him.

"How's your dog?" I ask as he's about to walk away.

Jake stops and turns around, smiling. "He's good. Working on his midair catches. Improving."

"Really? I'd like to see that sometime." I realize as I speak my mind that what I said could be construed as a request for another date. And since I don't want to lead him on with one of those, I try to fix it. "I mean, I've always been fascinated by canine athletes."

He laughs. "Really."

I throw a rag he left behind at him. "Shush."

He catches the rag and sticks it in his back pocket. "You're welcome to join us anytime. Just shoot me a text over the weekend, and I'll let you know the next time we're going to be out."

"Okay."

He's about to leave again, but something makes me stop him. "Hey."

When he turns, I feel uncomfortable, but I continue because I feel like I owe it to him. "You know that night you came over and Rob showed up?"

He nods, his expression back to serious. "Yep."

"I just ... wanted to explain."

"You don't need to."

"No, I know. But I want to." I stare at the ground, trying to work up the courage to say what needs to be said. "He's not my boyfriend."

"Okay."

"He never was, actually." I look up and laugh bitterly. "I wanted him to be, for a really long time. Like, since before I was a teenager." How silly I was. "He was my brother's college roommate, and then after he went to law school, he became our attorney for family matters and other things that came up."

Jake leans on the doorframe listening.

"When my brother Jeremy came back after his period of mourning or whatever, my other brother James said that Rob should decide if Jeremy was ready to be a father to Cassie. At the time, I kind of saw it as Rob making the decision personally, but I came to realize later that it was Rob just giving us a legal opinion about what the court would think." I realize as I explain this to Jake that somewhere along the way, I took his advice and started looking at what happened from a different perspective. I made a different choice. It's kind of empowering when I realize it.

Jake nods. "Makes sense."

"Does it?" I search his face for answers. He seems so... wise. The expression never to judge a book by its cover dances in my brain. A hot plumber dispensing excellent life advice; who would've thought?

"Based on what you've said and what I saw that night, he doesn't strike me as the kind of guy who would do something to deliberately hurt you."

"He's not. He's definitely not."

Jake shrugs. First he looks at the ground and then he looks up at me. "I know it's none of my business, but for what it's worth, I don't think you're the only one who's been thinking about you two being together. You and Rob, I mean."

"What?" I'm confused.

"That guy. Rob. I saw him that night and how he was looking at you. He thought we'd slept together. He wasn't happy."

I shake my head. "He's just protective. Like an older brother."

"No older brother looks at a sister like that. Trust me."

My heart starts racing over the idea. Now I have two people saying the same thing about Rob. Could it be true? "He came up to my apartment that night after you left and then ended up having some sort of ulcer attack and had to leave in an ambulance."

Jake's eyes bug out. "Seriously?"

I laugh. "Yes. Seriously." It does sound even crazier saying it out loud to someone. "When he was lying on the floor thinking he was dying, he said stuff. Like about what you said." I'm too embarrassed to say it. Rob kind of did declare some feelings for me. I'm still not sure what they were, though. Not that it matters now since he's not speaking to me anymore.

Jake nods. "Lucky guy."

I shake my head. "No. He's not even talking to me now."

Jake stands, no longer leaning on the doorframe. "Why not?"

I shrug, falling into the memory of my brother in the ER cubicle. "James. My brother. He told him to back off, and Rob said he would. James told me to back off too."

"And you just agreed to do it? After dreaming about the guy for twenty years?"

"Yeah. Pretty much. That's what the big boss of the whole world told me to do, and I did it." I'm acting like I'm twelve again, but James makes me feel that way often. He's always been able to become my parent when the mood struck him, and I've always just let it happen.

Jake comes into the bathroom and takes me by the hands, forcing me to look up at him. "Choices," he says. "Life's all about the choices you make."

"So you said before." I'm not mocking him; I'm more making fun of myself. Turns out, he's kind of right. I shouldn't have been so quick to dismiss his friend's wisdom before.

"You're choosing to let your brother make decisions for the both of you. Is that what you really want?"

"No." Looking into Jake's pretty eyes, I almost feel like I'm being mesmerized. "But I texted Rob and he didn't answer."

"What did your text say?"

"I said I wanted to talk."

Jake's mouth goes up in a half smile. "Not very bold, was it?"

I have to laugh. "No. Maybe not."

"Is this the same girl who threatened to knock my eye out with a samosa?"

My face goes pink. "I don't know."

He squeezes my hands and winks. "It is. I see her in there. She just needs to wake up and grow a pair."

I look down at my crotch. "I'm not sure I'd be able to fit a pair into these skinny jeans."

He leans back and laughs really loud. When he recovers, he pulls me into a hug. "You're killing me." He rubs my back and then leans to the side a little to look at me. "If I can't have you, then I need to hope at least this guy Rob can have a fair chance. Seems like he deserves you after being the object of your twenty-year crush. Otherwise, I'm going to start thinking there's no hope left in the world for guys like me."

I lose my smile as we step away from each other. "I'm sorry, Jake. I don't know what my problem is." He's such a great guy. Why couldn't I fall for someone like him?

"You don't have a problem."

I throw my arms up at him. "Of course I do! Look at you! You're perfect."

Now he looks like he's going red in the face. "Perfect? Hardly."

I punch him in the shoulder. "Come on. You know you are. You're smart, funny, gorgeous…" I pause, waiting to see if what I'm saying is penetrating.

"Keep going…" he says, gesturing with his hand in circles.

I laugh again. "Seriously. You'll find the right girl one of these days. I know you will. And I'll go to the wedding and see you standing there all hot in your tuxedo and curse the day I didn't jump your bones when I had the chance."

He smiles, but there's a hint of sadness to it. "Consider yourself at the top of the guest list."

We walk out of the bathroom together and into the dust-covered living room

"You going to call him?" he asks.

"Maybe," I say, shrugging. My heart is going crazy again as I picture the conversation Rob and I could have. Now that I'm admitting how I feel about him out loud to another person, and now that Jake's practically convinced me that Rob's feelings for me are mutual, it almost seems like something amazing could happen. The dream I've been dreaming since the day I saw Rob's picture could come true. It's like living on the edge of a fairy tale. Or maybe I'm standing at the edge of a cliff; it's kind of hard to tell since the symptoms of dizziness and rapid heart rate are the same.

"I dare you," he says. "Make a different choice than the one you've been making. What's the worst that could happen? Something different than what's been happening? That's good, right?"

I pull my phone out and stare at it. "I don't know. I really don't."

He shrugs, walking toward the front door. "Let me know how doing the same thing every day and expecting a different result works out for ya."

I grab a piece of drywall off the floor and throw it at his back, but he's out the door too fast to get hit by it.

I stare at my phone, wondering if I should take the risk.

Chapter Twenty-Six

I TRY ROB'S CELL PHONE first and get his voicemail. Pressing my lips together, I look at my screen. I could try his office. He often works late, and I have his inside line right here at my fingertips.

I press the button before I can second-guess myself. *Here goes nothing.* I listen as the line begins to ring.

"Arnold."

Rob answering with his last name throws me off. "Uh, hi," I finally say.

He doesn't respond for the longest time. I start to check my screen to see whether I still have a connection, but he speaks again and I put the phone back to my ear really quick.

"Hello. Who is this?"

God, I love his voice so much! Even when I don't know how he's feeling when he speaks, I still would rather listen to him than anyone else in the entire world. Emotions roll around in my head like a tornado, swirling around and around. Is he rejecting me? Telling me he knows who it is but giving me a chance to walk away without hearing the words that he doesn't want to talk to me ever again? Or does he really not recognize my voice after all these years of talking to me on the phone? Has he cut me out of his life that thoroughly? I'd know his voice anywhere.

I don't know how to react. I could joke. I could act cool. I could hang up. What's the right thing to do? Why did I call? What the hell is wrong with me?

"Uhhh..." I can't get anything else out. I think I'm going to throw up. Why did I listen to Jake? He has no idea what he's talking about. He's a convicted felon for God's sake!

"Jana, is it you?"

I breathe out a huge sigh of relief when he doesn't sound angry. "Yes, it's me. I'm sorry."

He says nothing for a few seconds.

I open my mouth to fill up the space, but he cuts me off.

"What are you apologizing for? You haven't done anything wrong."

"I called you." As if that makes any sense at all. Why *am* I apologizing?

"Yeah, you did." He sounds disappointed. I want to crawl in a hole and never come out.

"I'm sorry." I try not to let my sadness come out in my voice.

"Would you stop apologizing, please?"

"I don't know what else to do!" I'm whining like a baby now. Forget being cool. Who am I kidding? I'm not cool. I'm never cool. I'm always awkward, always faking it, always dreaming about a man I can't have. Argh! I hate this!

He chuckles. "Well, if you ask your brother, he'd tell you that you have to hang up your phone right this instant."

I speak between gritted teeth. "If I had a dart board, I would put his picture on it and throw darts at it until it fell into shreds on my floor."

He laughs really loudly and finishes with a sigh. I can hear the smile in his voice. "Can I come play darts with you?"

Suddenly my whole body is warm. "Yes, you can. Anytime."

The line goes silent, but I'm not going to be the one to say the first word now that the walls are coming down. I'm too afraid I'll say the wrong thing and throw them right back up again.

"So where do we go from here?" Rob finally asks.

I bite my lip. "I don't know." Please say you like me, please say you like me, please don't be playing games with my heart!

"Maybe you should let me take you out on a real date."

Screaming silently, I throw my arms wide and dance around the room, making myself dizzy with the spinning, spinning, spinning…

"Hello? Hello?" I hear a tiny voice coming from the end of my arm.

"Hi," I say, throwing the phone up to my ear again. "Sorry about that. Dropped the phone thingy."

"That shocking, huh?" He sounds sad.

"Shocking? Nooo, no, not shocking." Do I dare say it? Say what I'm really feeling? Take the risk of sounding like an idiot? Aw, what the hell. Why not? "More like exciting."

The smile is back in his voice again. "When?"

I'm almost out of breath. "Friday." That gives me three days to find the perfect outfit and freak out completely. I'll probably even grow some pimples if I'm really lucky. Ack! Already freaking out!

"Friday it is. Seven o'clock? I'll pick you up?"

I don't trust myself not to totally jump his bones if he's that close to my bedroom, so I shake my head. "No. I'll meet you."

"Hmmm. Not sure if I like that."

I'm flicking my hand around, trying to get rid of the tingly feeling in my fingers. For some reason I'm still out of breath. "Just do it."

"Fine. You're the boss. Where?"

"You pick." Now I'm hopping up on my toes, making my calves burn with the unusual exercise. I have all this excess energy that's ready to explode out of me. I think I could run a marathon right now and win.

"Hmmm. The pressure. Not sure I can hack it."

I practice some booty muscle squeezes, wondering if I can raise my buttcheeks a half inch by Friday if I really put my mind to it. "I think you can. Text me with your choice by tomorrow." I have to quit with the cheek-squeezing when I get a cramp that makes my leg buckle. I have to grab the nearby kitchen counter to keep from going down.

"I can't have until Friday?"

"No, of course not," I say, massaging my butt muscle and wincing. "I have to shop."

"Well, all right then. I'll text you by tomorrow."

"Good." I bend over in half at the waist, wondering if we'll end up having sex. I'm going to have to stretch all my leg muscles for the next three days to make sure I'm limber enough to impress him. I might only get one shot at this thing.

"Good," he says.

I smile. "Fine." I'm standing now, tracing hearts on the countertop in the dust with my finger as the sweat pours out of me.

"Fine," he says.

"Stop copying me." I put his initials on top of mine and draw a heart around them both.

"I'm not copying you. You're copying me."

"I'm hanging up now." I add an arrow to my heart drawing.

"No, I'm hanging up now."

I wait but nothing happens. "I'm doing it."

"So am I."

I want to curl up in a bed and draw hearts and flowers all over a notebook with his initials and my first name attached to his last name and all the silly things I used to do when I was in high school and dreamed of being his girlfriend.

"Goodbye, Jana."

"Goodbye, Robinson."

"I really hate it when you call me that," he says.

My cheeks go warm when I realize what he means. "Goodbye, *Rob*."

His voice comes back soft and warm. Sexy. "That's better."

My face is flaming red when I finally hang up two seconds

later. I have to scream with all my might to get rid of all the crazy energy that's making me feel like I'm going to explode at any second. I hope none of my new neighbors hears me and calls the cops. But if they do, who cares? I'll just tell them that I'm in love and they'll have to understand. A love like this doesn't come around all that often.

Chapter Twenty-Seven

O F COURSE FRIDAY TOOK FOREVER to get here. I stand in front of my mirror, checking my new outfit from all angles. The dark blue and black dress fits me to a T, the low neckline showing off what little cleavage I have to its best advantage. The necklace my parents gave me for my college graduation sits right in the center of my chest, the diamonds and sapphire winking in the light of my bedroom. The black heels are gorgeous; I just hope there's no ice on the sidewalks tonight or I'm definitely going to go down.

I don't wear my hair up all that often, but I remember the one time Rob ever commented on my 'do, and it was a day I had it in a clip. Ten years later, the memory is as crisp as if he'd said it yesterday: "Your hair looks good like that." Not the most eloquent words ever used, but they stuck with me and made me feel beautiful for a really long time. Every time I put my hair up after that, even if it was just in a ponytail, I felt sexy.

The fact that I remember something so inconsequential and let it guide how I view myself tells me that Rob's had a very strong influence on my life for a long time — more than I realized before. I just hope that the reality of being with him lives up to the decade and a half of dreaming I've done.

Ugh, the pressure I'm putting on myself is killing me. I had to buy some heavy duty cover-up at Sephora yesterday when the first of three new zits popped up on my chin. I glare at them in the mirror, but so far can't see them under the three layers of blemish-erasing creams. I have the tubes in my purse just in case.

My phone beeps and a message from Leah pops up.

What are you doing tonight? Can I stop by?

I feel guilty. I haven't told her anything, worried she'll let it slip to James what Rob and I are up to. It's not that I think my brother has the right to control my life, but I figured it's better if Rob and I see if this thing will even work out before we get my brother all riled up about it.

Working. Maybe tomorrow?

I toy with the pieces of curled hair hanging down by my ears as I wait for her response.

I thought you'd say that. Buzz Buzz.

Buzz buzz? What's that mean? Is that a new internet saying I haven't learned yet? I'm about to type out some question marks in response when my intercom goes off. I stand there in my room with my eyes going round. Is it Rob? I told him I'd meet him at the restaurant he chose. If he comes up here, I know I'm going to be tempted to drag him into my bedroom. Ack! I'm not ready!

I rush to the door and press the intercom button. "Yes?"

"Hey, hey, hey! It's me! Let me in."

Oh my god, it's *Leah*. Dammit! I press the button to let her in and speak simultaneously. "I'm on my way out. You can come up for two seconds."

She doesn't answer, probably already halfway down the hall. Pregnancy hasn't slowed her down one bit.

I stand in the entrance to my apartment with the door open, my purse over my shoulder and keys in my hand. Hopefully, Leah will get the hint.

A minute or two later, the elevator doors open and she steps off, her face lighting up when she sees me. Then she frowns in confusion. "I thought you said you were working." She stops a few feet away, her eyes going wide. "Tell me you're not a prostitute."

My jaw drops open in shock as a laugh bursts out of me. "Oh my god, you just said I look like a hooker." I'm not sure it's a bad thing where Rob and this whole first date thing is concerned, though, so I'm okay with the reference. Maybe if he's too busy noticing how sexy I look, he'll forget how many times he saw me as his younger sister.

She rushes at me with her arms open and flings herself into me, belly first. "I'm sorry! I didn't mean it like that! You look amazing!"

I pat her on the back, sucking in my gut to give her baby more room to breathe between us.

She yanks her body backwards, keeping her hands on my upper arms. Her eyes are narrowed. "Where are you really going? I know you're not working. Are you going out on a date?"

"Maybe." I search her face, trying to decide if I can trust her with the truth or if I should just feed her a lie.

"Awesome." She grins big. "You've been acting like a nun for way too long."

I have to smile at that. "How would you know? I haven't seen you in ages."

"Are you telling me you've been having sex every night of the week?"

"Hardly."

"So who's your hot date?" She backs up so she can look at me from head to toe. "Someone you must like a whole lot if that dress is any indication. And those shoes! Oh my. You'd better hang onto his arm. It's cold out there."

My face is turning pink again. I sigh, frustrated that I'm so easy to read. "I'll tell you but only if you promise not to tell James."

"You don't have to tell me. I already know." She squeals and grabs me into another hug. "I'm so happy for you guys."

"Thanks. I think." I pat her on the back again.

She steps away and sighs. "It's Rob, right?"

I nod, afraid if I say anything else I'll ruin my makeup. Tears are ever-present where this situation is concerned. Too many emotions, so little time…

"I knew it!" She looks over my shoulder toward my door. "Are you going to invite me in?"

"I really can't. I was just about to leave. I'm supposed to meet him at Eleven Madison Park." I feel terrible. Now that she's here, I realize how much I miss talking to her, especially about things like this.

"Holy moly, hotsy totsy. He must really want to get in your panties." She gestures at my dress. "Good thing you're making it easy for him. That'll make him happy."

"I'd slap you right now, but you're pregnant." I step forward and give her a hug instead.

"I prefer this anyway." She rubs my back. "You have fun, okay? Don't worry about James. I'll handle his bossy butt, don't you worry."

I laugh as I release her. "I'm sure you will." I look her in the eye so she'll know how much I mean my next words. "I'm really glad I have you in my corner. And I'm glad James has you too. He really needed you to come into his life when you did."

"You're telling me. I finally met that hag he was dating before. What a piece of work she is."

My eyes widen. "You did? What happened?" This might be worth being late to dinner over. To say I wasn't a fan of that wench would be an understatement, but unlike my bossy brother James, I never stuck my nose into his business and told him she was wrong for him.

Leah turns to the elevator and presses the button. "I'll tell you over lunch. Are you free tomorrow?"

I grab my coat just inside my front door and lock up, hurrying to join her at the elevator. "I'll get free for you. Just text me the details of where and when you want to meet."

She waits for me to get in and then releases the hold button, sending us down to the lobby. "Fair warning; I'm going to invite James."

I frown, my mood instantly deflating. "I'm not coming."

"Yes, you are. I'm inviting him so we can all talk and get this over with." She sighs, shaking her head. "So much time wasted on being silly. I never realized how awesome having a brother could be until I met Ralph. I don't want to waste a single moment where he's concerned. You guys are lucky. You've known each other your whole lives; but that doesn't mean you get to be stupid and throw that relationship to the side whenever it gets difficult."

I stare at her as she watches the elevator light up the next lowest floor. I could swear sometimes I hear a ghost speaking from her lips. "You remind me so much of Laura."

"Really?" Leah grins at me. "That's a high compliment."

"It is." I smile, looking at our reflection in the elevator doors. "She was awesome. Very insightful."

"Boo says I'm like her, but on crack."

I have to laugh at that. He's right. But that nickname... "I can't believe you call him Boo." It's so completely crazy. Who would look at my brother, the most put together, serious, brainiac butt-head in the world, and see a *Boo*? Only Leah, that's who. She's perfect for him. I can't wait to see how their baby turns out.

We reach the lobby and walk across it to the front doors together. Leah throws the end of her scarf over her shoulder and smiles at me. "Good luck tonight."

"Thanks." I'm nervous all over again. Dammit. I'm probably sprouting another pimple.

"And whatever you do, don't worry about what James will think or say. He doesn't matter in this equation. It's just you and Rob. One plus one equals One."

I hold the door open for her and give her the first cab that comes by. As I close the door on her, she smiles and gives me a thumbs up through the window. I'm still laughing when I get into my cab and head over to one of the swankiest restaurants in Manhattan to meet the man of my dreams.

Chapter Twenty-Eight

ROB IS WAITING FOR ME at the bar. I'd recognize the shape and breadth of his shoulders anywhere. His hair looks freshly cut. I wonder if he did that for me. He doesn't see me at first, so I take a few seconds to ogle. If I didn't know him and just happened to see him as a stranger from across the room, I'd do the same thing — stare like some kind of creeper. There's just something about him that draws my eye, makes me want to get to know him, makes me wonder what's going on inside that head of his. His profile shows off his strong jaw and his nose with the bump in it from a sports accident of some sort. My brother has teased him about it for years, always offering to fix it for him. My heart fills with warmth as Rob turns to look at me and his eyes light up in recognition.

I've walked on heels since I was fifteen, but you'd never know it as I try to make my way across the room. I trip not once, but twice, on invisible bumps in the floor. For my second one, I'm just a foot away from my destination. Rob's arm comes out to catch me, and I land against his side.

The ice in his glass chinks around as he steadies us both. "Well, hello there," he says, amused. "That's one way to make an entrance."

"Oh my god," I say, my face beet red. "I've forgotten how to walk, I guess."

"Are you sure you're not just making a move on me?"

I stand on my own power and smile, praying he can't see my zits. I'm afraid I rubbed off some of my cream on his jacket, but the lighting is too low to know for sure. "Please. I have to believe I'm smoother than that."

He signals the bartender and then looks at me. "What'll you have?"

You in my bed?

"Umm, how about some white wine. Whatever's good." My face is still flushed. Now that I'm finally here on a date with my dream-guy, it feels like I've left the real world and entered one of my daydreams. How many have I created over the years? A hundred? Two hundred. No, not even close. It's probably more like a thousand.

He orders for me and hands me the glass, lifting his own at the same time. "Here's to first dates, as awkward as they are."

I touch my glass to his. "Here's hoping I get more coordinated as the night goes on."

I nearly choke on my wine when he winks at me and says, "I'll drink to that."

As he sips his whiskey, I look around the room in an effort to stop staring at him. Every other time in my life when I've stood next to him, I've been chatting about inane stuff, or commenting about some family matter or something my brothers might have done. But now we're together because we're mutually interested in seeing whether we can have any kind of relationship that doesn't focus on or feature my brothers in any way. I feel like I'm about to have a stroke. I have no idea what to say or what to talk about.

"You ready to sit at a table?" he asks. He's all calm and collected, showing no sign of being freaked out. I think they taught him that skill in law school or something.

My eyes dart around the room as I take in all the people having quiet conversations, the tall ceilings going up to forever, the waiters bustling around serving up food people will talk about for years after leaving... and I just can't picture it. I can't picture me sitting there with Rob and having our first date.

"What's wrong?" he asks, putting his hand on my elbow.

"Nothing." My voice comes out really high, so I rein it in and try again. "Nothing. I'm fine. Why would you ask me that? Don't I look fine?" I reach up and almost touch my chin, but stop myself just in time and touch my hair instead, patting the side of it. That's all I need to do is call his attention to the pimple factory. I've never felt so uncomfortable in my own skin as I do right now.

Rob touches my cheek with one finger and then pulls it away. "Jana. I've known you forever. I know your panicked look when I see it."

I war within myself over whether I should be honest and admit what I'm feeling or fake it until I make it. And in this case, *make it* could mean have an actual panic attack and run from the room screaming or just stumble my way through dinner the way I did my entrance. Either way, it's not going to be pretty.

"Come on," he says all of a sudden. "Let's get out of here." He puts his drink on the bar top.

"What?" I'm confused.

He takes my wine glass, puts it next to his tumbler, and then throws forty bucks after it. "I changed my mind. I don't want to eat here." He starts leading me toward the exit.

"What do you mean?" I look up at him, worried he's angry or changing his mind about being with me. Were my pimples that horrible that they completely put him off the idea of being with me? I knew I should have bought more cover-up.

"This was a bad idea. Coming here. I should have kept it more low-key."

"Low key, like... as friends?" I hate how weepy my voice sounds.

He stops all of a sudden, making me crash into the back of him. When he turns around his eyes have a crazy look to them.

"Please tell me you're joking."

He looks as sick as I felt thinking it. I smile and squeeze his hand. "Ignore me. I'm nervous." And now I'm flying on a cloud! Because I can tell from his expression that he wants to be with me as much as I want to be with him. Or he wants to be with me as more than a friend, at least. I can build on that. Hell, I've built an entire imaginary life as his wife, spent years perfecting that vision. I can do this.

"I know, and it's my fault. This restaurant will be great for our fifth date, but not our first." He stops at the front and retrieves our coats and scarves.

He said fifth date! Weeee!

"Where are we going?" I ask, excited about the change of venue. He's right. This place is too stuffy for us right now. Not that I know the right place for us on our first date. And he said fifth date! Weeeee again!

"Just trust me." He stops just before walking out the door. "You trust me, don't you?"

I nod, taking his hand and folding my fingers through his. "Yes. I trust you with everything."

He leans down and kisses me just to the left of my mouth. "Good." He turns toward the exit and lifts his hand, like he's going to push the door open.

I stop him with a hand on his sleeve.

He looks down at me, a bemused smile on his face.

"Try that again," I say, staring at his lips.

"Try what again?"

"That kiss. I think you missed."

I can tell the exact moment that he gets what I'm after. His eyes go warm and he turns toward me, a hand coming up to touch the side of my face. He leans down and I catch a whiff of whiskey on his breath before his lips are fully pressed against mine.

My heart soars and my head nearly explodes with the feelings that rush through me the moment we touch. His lips fit so perfectly against mine. I expected awkwardness. Fumbling around. A banging of noses and teeth. But none of that happens. Instead, his tongue comes out to slide across my bottom lip a second before he pulls away. It's way more amazing than I ever dreamed it could be.

"That better?" he asks me.

I nod dumbly afraid if I try to speak it'll just come out as a disjointed flow of random syllables.

He frowns. "I can do better. I promise."

I smile as he pushes the door open and a blast of winter air hits us. I can't feel the cold right now, though. I'm impervious to its effects. Rob's kiss has warmed me all the way down to my toes, and I'm pretty sure I'm not even walking on the pavement right now. Every step I take feels like I'm floating an inch above everyone else's feet. No man's kiss has ever made me feel this way. I'm almost afraid of what will happen when he really gets his hands on me.

Sex with Rob! Ahhh! I've fallen into a rabbit hole and I never want to come out!

"Taxi!" Rob adds a whistle to his call and a cab zooms from the other lane to reach us.

As we settle into our seats, the cabbie looks into his mirror. "Where to?"

Rob speaks up without hesitation. "Times Square. Stardust Diner."

I sit back in the seat, eagerly awaiting my first adventure with Rob. I have no idea what this diner is all about, but so long as he's there and he kisses me again, I'm all for it.

Rob's fingers weave in with mine and we rest our hands on the seat between us. I cannot stop grinning the entire way across the city.

Chapter Twenty-Nine

THERE'S A LINE OUTSIDE THE Stardust diner that looks like any other restaurant of its kind. Usually when I see a group of people waiting to get inside a place, I turn around and head the other direction, especially when it's cold out. Tonight, it's a different matter altogether. Time spent in line is more time for Rob to kiss me. We take our places at the back of the group and stand, face to face. Rob wraps his arms around my waist and smiles at me.

"Have you ever been here before?"

"No." I glance at the people next to me. They seem pretty excited, but it's hard to tell if it's because of the restaurant or the fact that they're tourists seeing Times Square for the first time.

"I think you'll like it."

The way he says it makes me suspicious. "Are there Chippendale dancers in there or something?"

He laughs and shakes his head. "What makes you think I frequent a diner that has half-naked men dancing around inside it?"

"Good point. But the way you said it... the way you asked me. You looked sneaky."

He adjusts his arms around me, bringing me a little closer. "Sneaky. I'm not sneaky. I'm the opposite of sneaky."

"Says who?" A glimmer of our recent history tries to sneak into my brain, but I tamp it down. I can't think of Cassie tonight; it'll ruin everything.

"Says anyone who's ever known me. I've tried my whole life to keep secrets and it never works. The truth is always written all over my face. That's why I mostly do contract law. I'd be slain in court."

I stare at that face he claims is an open book and shake my head. "Sorry. Nope. I have no idea what you're thinking right now."

His expression changes to something more serious. "Why is it that the person who's actually seen my face more than almost anyone else is the one least able to read it?"

I shrug. "I have no idea. Maybe I'm just bad at it."

He sighs. "Or maybe I've spent way too much energy trying to keep things from you over the years and I've gotten really good at it."

"What do you mean?" My voice has gone soft because it feels like I'm about to hear a confession of sorts. I don't want to discourage him; we both need to clear the air about a few things before we can move forward. I'm just not sure the line for the Stardust Diner is the best place for all of that. A glance to my left tells me we're about two parties behind the front of the line.

"Do you remember when we first met?" he asks.

"How could I forget?" My cheeks start to burn with the admission, but I can't stop smiling. Tonight will be a night of taking risks, telling truths that have stayed hidden for a really long time.

"I came back with your brother for Christmas break."

"Oh, believe me, I remember every detail." My heart grows full with memories of myself dreaming of him over the years. That first day I saw him, I knew. I knew he'd play the starring role in my dreams forever.

"So do I. You were wearing shorts and a rainbow unicorn T-shirt. You were just a kid."

I frown. "Shorts? It was winter time."

"I know. You were dancing around in your room or something. You came running down the stairs in shorts and a T-shirt, with your hair in a ponytail. You told James you were going to be a cheerleader when you were older and you had to start learning the moves now."

"Oh my god, I forgot that part." A flash of Rob at the bottom of the stairs comes to me. "I was so mad at James for not warning me you were coming."

The corner of Rob's mouth quirks up in a smile. "You were mad at him? Why?"

I sigh, trying not to grin but finding it impossible. "He sent a picture of the two of you home with one of his letters. I'm afraid to admit I got a little nuts over that thing."

"Reeeally? When you were that young? Tell me more."

His silly grin makes me want to smack him or kiss him, I can't decide which. I keep talking instead of choosing between the two. "I don't know. I just saw you and you were wearing that crew shirt and you guys had your arms around each other and..." I shrug. It seems silly to say it out loud.

"What? Tell me." He leans in closer, shutting out the world. "I won't tell anyone."

"I thought you said you were terrible at keep secrets."

"Not all secrets. Just the ones that should be shared."

"That makes no sense."

"Stop stalling and tell me the rest of the story about how you fell in love with my picture."

"Hey! I didn't say I fell in love with your picture." I try to push him away, but he stays put, holding me tighter. I feel silly with him smiling at me like that.

"Come on, just admit it," he says.

"No. I'm not admitting anything." I pout, trying to move past my silly emotions. He could devastate me so easily. One wrong word and I could go from happy and confident to destroyed. I feel like I'm standing near the edge of a cliff being urged to move a little closer to it.

"Okay, I'll start." He leans down and kisses me briefly on the lips, pulling away before we can really get into it. "The first time I saw you, I thought of you like a kid sister. That vacation, you were with us everywhere. James was annoyed, but I thought it was cute. I didn't have any siblings, as you know, so having a little girl running around bugging us was funny to me. And you were so comical. I was constantly laughing at the things you were saying, but James just got madder and madder. I didn't care that you were always there. I liked it."

My heart lurches, like it's flipped over in my chest cavity. The smile on my face gets even bigger. "Really?" That he had the patience for a little girl as an eighteen year old teenager is amazing. I remember my brother trying to shut me out of his bedroom and our mother forcing him to let me stay.

"Really. James hated that I liked having you around. I think he was jealous or something. Not that he was in love with me or anything, but I think he had more exciting things planned for our break than babysitting his annoying little sister. After the first week, he did everything he could to keep me away from you."

"I didn't notice."

He laughs. "Of course you didn't. Because no matter what he did, you showed up anyway."

I can't look Rob in the eyes now. I remember hounding them over the years like some kind of crazy hunting dog on a scent. When I got to my pre-teen and early teen years, I'd ask my parents where James was going, they'd tell me, and I'd pretend like I was planning to go there too and get my mom or my dad to drop me off or force James to chaperone me.

"The country club, the mall, the golf course, even."

"And I hated golf too," I add, kind of proud of my determination at such a young age. I'm going to try and convince myself it was that and not the early budding stage of a stalker.

"You were terrible at it, I remember that."

"Hey!" I play smack him on the chest. "I wasn't that bad."

"You hit the side of our cart with a ball from the tee.

"It was a bad slice."

"James was convinced you were trying to put him in the hospital."

"He was always overly dramatic."

"Your brother? Overly dramatic? On what planet?"

"Whatever. He just didn't want to share you, but I did." I shrug. "Not my problem."

"I'm glad you made him share. Over the years we both got used to it. And after I saw you in your bathing suit when you were seventeen, I didn't want to hang out with him anymore anyway."

"What? You're crazy." I want to jump out from his arms and dance and sing, but I restrain myself. Barely.

"It was yellow and pink. Bright colors. And each side had this tassel thing hanging down. You were way too young for me, but I couldn't help staring."

"Wow, your attention to detail is amazing."

He leans in and whispers in my ear. "I remember other things about you in that suit too, but I'm keeping it clean since we're in public." His lips touch my neck and he kisses me. A shiver moves out from there to cover my entire body.

"Next!" a voice from off to my left says loudly.

We both look up suddenly, as if we've been caught doing something we shouldn't have.

A lady is standing there with a clipboard in both hands. "You coming in or staying out here?" She smiles.

"On our way." Rob takes my hand in his and guides me into the restaurant. I'm glad for the support because otherwise, I'd probably just float right up into the ether and set the sky on fire.

Chapter Thirty

THE PLACE IS HOPPING. THERE must be three hundred people inside, from all walks of life. It's impossible to tell how many are tourists and how many are locals. We get a seat right in the center of everything, sitting shoulder-to-shoulder with other people at tables so close I could reach over and sneak french fries from their plates.

"You've been here before?" I ask.

"Once." He looks down at his menu.

"Was it a date?"

"Yes." He doesn't look up.

Jealousy like I've never known comes rising up from the depths and feels like it's strangling me. I want to kill this woman, whoever she is. Obviously, I've gone completely mental, now that I have my prize nearly in my grasp. I should probably stop asking questions and convince myself that jealously like this is a bad idea, but I don't. Of course I don't.

"Do I know her? What's her name?"

"Yes, you know her." He frowns at the menu, like he's concentrating really hard on it.

I lift my own menu a little and move it across the table to tap on his with it. He finally looks up, acting all innocent like he wasn't just trying to hide from me.

"What's her name?"

He stares at me for a few seconds before answering. "Does it matter?"

I wasn't sure before, but now I am. "Yes. It matters to me."

"I'm not seeing her anymore. I went out with her twice. That's it. It was never serious."

"Just waiting for a name," I say, smiling. I'm pretty sure my expression is a little strained, but the more he plays hard to get, the more worried I become.

He opens his mouth to say something, but a voice coming out over a loudspeaker interrupts him.

"Are we ready for a little noise?" the person asks, obviously expecting a positive response.

I look around, confused as to what's going on. There's a table of women across the room from me who are waving long strips of white paper around. It's then that I notice a server with a roll of register tape running from table to table, ripping off two-foot lengths of it and giving them to other diners.

I lean over and ask my date, "What the heck?" but before Rob can answer, the voice is back, and now there's music pumping out of the sound system.

"Aw, yeah, baby! Let me introduce to you... tonight, back from his Broadway debut... Johnny Blakely!" The girls at the other table start yelling and waving their register tape even more enthusiastically. And then off to my right some guy starts jumping up and down and singing into the microphone. I recognize Macklemore's *Can't Hold Us* immediately.

Rob starts to grin, and I smile like a fool. I had no idea we were going to be treated to a show with our meals. When the waiter behind me hands me some register tape, I take it and start waving it around enthusiastically with everyone else.

The entire place is hopping with the beat. I can feel the bass in my bones. The singing waiter jumps up on the back of the booth

Rob is sitting in and does a rap duo with another server across the room. Lights are flashing, and a chorus line of other servers starts up; they're dancing in synch to the rhythm set by the two rapper guys, the music, and all us diners stomping our feet.

I start yelling for the sheer joy of it, and I'm not the only one. It's crazy; like I've entered into another dimension where yelling at the top of your lungs and waving paper around is completely acceptable behavior in a restaurant.

By the time they finish, they're covered in sweat and I'm exhausted. There's more yammering going on over the mic but I can't focus on anything but Rob now.

"Did you know that was going to happen?" Why am I out of breath? I have no idea. I'm not the one who was performing, but it feels like I was.

"The singing? Yeah. It happens all the time. You'll hear more."

I look at the guy who was just rapping his butt off, who's now calmly serving drinks at a table nearby. "More? How can they possibly keep that up all night?"

"It won't be him singing all the time. They take turns."

"They?" I'm wondering if they hire performers and mix them in with the other servers.

"Everyone who works here is a Broadway hopeful. They all can sing and dance, and they take turns. Usually it's musical numbers, but not always."

I have more questions, but they'll have to wait because our server's here and he wants to know what we're ordering. After some hemming and hawing I settle for a chicken wrap and then stare at my date while another song starts, this one from *Les Miserables*.

"This is the most interesting first date I've ever had."

"It doesn't feel so much like a first date anymore," Rob says, leaning forward and taking my hand. He rests it on the table as he gazes at me.

I swear it hurts to look at him this close and know he's here with me. He's so beautiful.

"What?" he asks, smiling.

"What?" I say back, feeling silly.

"What are you thinking? You have the cutest expression on your face."

"Nothing."

"Liar."

"Fine, you want to know? I was thinking how gorgeous you are. And how I can't believe I'm sitting here across from you after thinking about doing it for so long."

"How long?" he asks, teasing me.

"Way too long." A little girl's crush turned into a teenager's obsession and eventually an adult woman's fantasy.

His teasing face falls away. "Me too. It's been too long." He tilts his head. "Tell me again why we waited to do this."

I shrug. "I had no idea you wanted to."

"How could you not know?"

"You never gave me any signals." I can clearly remember thinking how one-sided the feelings were. He smiled at me and was polite, but I never caught him looking at me or trying to get close to me.

"That's because your brother would have killed me."

"Why? Why is he so against us being together?"

"I guess a lot of his friends started going after you once you got some curves, and he was starting to think that's the only reason anyone came around to hang out with him anymore."

"That's not true." This is the first I'm hearing of this. I think Rob's fooling himself.

"It absolutely is. And he's warned me in no uncertain terms that I'm not to go near you. More than once."

I sit back in my chair, my hand sliding from Rob's. "And you listened to him?"

"I listened before, but I'm not now, am I?" He pauses. "What's wrong? Are you mad?"

I shrug. "I'm not sure. Maybe."

"At me or James?"

"James, mostly. Why would he do that? Why would he interfere in my life like that? In my happiness?"

Rob's expression changes. It happens so fast and then it's gone, I almost can believe I imagined it. But when his jaw tightens once really fast after, I know I didn't.

"What?" I ask. "What's wrong?"

Rob shakes his head. "Now's not the time to discuss it."

"When?" I ask, getting cranky.

"When what?"

"When will be the time to discuss it?"

Rob stares into my eyes for a long time. "After dinner. I promise."

I nod once. "Fine. After dinner, then." I try to smile and move past the moment, but it's impossible. Now there's some kind of weird dark shadow hanging over our table that won't go away. Our dinner is delivered, and I manage to eat some of it, but when they ask if we want coffee or dessert I decline and ask for the check.

"Anxious to leave?" Rob asks, putting his napkin on the table next to his plate.

"Anxious to get to the bottom of your story," I say, standing as the bill arrives.

"Are you sure you want to do this? Get into all these details before we have a chance to enjoy ourselves for a while?" He helps me get into my coat as the mood grows even darker.

"I'm sure." We walk out of the diner into the cold night air. Rob hails a taxi and I follow him inside. He gives the address for his apartment, but I don't say a word. Might as well get to the bottom of things, so I can decide whether I'm going to keep singing Rob's praises and my good fortune or start planning the rest of my life without him in it.

Chapter Thirty-One

I HAVE ONLY BEEN TO Rob's place a few times in my life. Today I'm seeing it for the first time as his girlfriend. Or his potential girlfriend. I have no idea what's going to happen in the next hour. We could end up in bed together, or I could be in a taxi going home and crying my eyes out. The stress of not knowing which one it will be is killing me.

"Here," Rob says, handing me a glass of something amber-colored.

"What's this?" I ask, taking a sniff of it. "Phew, that's strong."

He takes a big gulp of his drink and points to the couch after. "Have a seat. And drink up. You're going to want to be buzzed for this."

My eyebrow goes up. "I'm going to want to be buzzed or *you're* going to want me buzzed?"

"Both." He takes me by the hand and pulls me over to the sitting area, dragging me down to the couch with him.

I take up a position two cushions away. I can't trust that I'll be smart about this conversation if he's any closer. He looks positively edible in his starched shirt with cufflinks and slacks.

He drinks more and stares off into space, a brooding look taking over his features.

"So, you said you went on a date to the diner with someone else," I say. "Who was it?"

He sighs and looks over at me. "You're still on that?"

"I'm still on anything that remains a secret between us."

"I've known you for over twenty years. That's a lot of secrets."

I shrug. "I've got time."

"The question is whether you have the patience. And forgiveness."

My eyes kind of bug out at that. "Forgiveness? Why? What have you done?"

He looks back at his glass, swirling the liquid around over the ice. "A few things I'm not exactly proud of. Things I wish I'd handled differently, I guess you could say."

"Like what, for instance?"

He looks over at me, suddenly sad. "Do we have to do this now? Can't we do it later? After?"

"After what?" I'm almost laughing, but I'm not happy.

I catch him glancing over toward a door across the room and realize he means after we go into his bedroom and have sex.

I put my drink on the table and look him right in the eye. "If you think I'm going to sleep with you when there are secrets between us, you'd better think again, Bud."

He grins, but it's not the happy kind. "Damn."

"Yeah. Damn. I know exactly what you're thinking now, so just get over yourself. I don't care how good you are in bed, I'm not letting this go. You owe me the truth."

He nods, staring into his drink again. "I suppose I do."

I lean back into the corner of the couch, easing my heels off and wiggling my formerly cramped toes. "Go ahead. I'm ready."

"Are you sure?" He's still not looking at me.

"Absolutely. But you better hurry up and just say it. The longer you wait, the worse it's getting in my head."

A long stretch of silence grows between us, but I wait. I'm not going to harass him. Either this relationship is worth a little hard work or it isn't. I'm done with hounding him and trying to force myself on him. If he wants me, he needs to come and get me.

"You asked me who I went to Stardust with before you."

"Yes, I did."

"I dated this woman twice. That's it. She wasn't anyone special to me."

"And her name is...?" I wait for his answer, growing less patient by the second.

He sighs heavily. "Her name is Hilary." He sneaks a glance at me, kind of ducking his shoulders.

"Hilary?"

He can't possibly mean the Hilary I know.

"Hilary? As in James's Hilary?" The woman he was with for a couple years and almost married? That can't be right.

"Yes. That Hilary."

I shake my head, confused. This isn't possible. "What do you mean you went out with Hilary twice? When?"

"When they broke up."

"Last year?"

He shakes his head. "No. A year before that."

"They broke up before that?" Still confused over here. I have no idea what he's talking about.

He takes another long drink from his glass, almost emptying it. Then he looks at me. "She called me up and told me all the terrible things James was doing. Working too late, not calling her. She thought he was having an affair, so she broke up with him."

"James having an affair? He would never do that."

"I know. I should have known. But I listened to her and I believed her."

"But why would she say that?"

"I have no idea. Maybe she really believed it. There's no way for me to know now. I haven't spoken to her since she and James got back together."

"Did you sleep with her?" I'm already mad, but not sure why. Am I jealous? Angry on my brother's behalf?

"No. I got close, I'm not going to lie to you, but I didn't go through with it."

"Why not?" I'm keeping a handle on my emotions. I'm pretty proud of myself, actually.

"Does it matter?" He looks tortured, but I don't care.

"To me it does."

"I didn't sleep with her because she was James's ex-girlfriend."

"Not because you didn't want to sleep with her," I clarify. "Not because she's an evil bitch or anything like that."

He shakes his head. "Men don't think about women like that."

"You're trying to tell me you can't identify an evil bitch when you see one in action? Because holy hell, I know you saw Hilary do her thing more than once. We all did." That woman … she was something else. I'm surprised she didn't run James over with her car when he finally ended things between them. She's that horrible.

"No, I'm saying that even when a woman like Hilary… does the things that Hilary does, it doesn't necessarily make her not attractive in certain ways."

I shake my head, disgusted with what I'm hearing. "I can't believe you. You're basically saying you would have slept with her, even though she's a horrible person."

"No, what I'm saying is that I went out with her a couple times, at her request, ostensibly to talk about James but also with the thought in the back of my mind that I might sleep with her. But when I realized she and James weren't really over, I backed off. I shouldn't have gone out with her in the first place, even if she and James were done for good. I know that. I *knew* that. I should have told her no. I knew better, but I did it anyway, and for that, I'm ashamed."

I mull over what he's said for a while. *Judge not, lest I be judged,* keeps running through my head like it's on a loop. As a result, I try to open my mind and my heart and see Rob for who he is: a man with urges like any other guy out there. Can I hate him for being that person? Do I want to be with a guy who never makes mistakes? Does such a man even exist? I know the answer already. I'm just going through the process I need to in order to forgive the idea of him with Hilary. She really is so, so awful.

"I don't understand how a guy who would go out with Hilary and think of sleeping with her would want to be with me." There, I said it. I not only compared myself to another of his potential girlfriends, I basically begged for some compliments. Well done, Stupid Self. Why don't you offer him a blowjob on the first date while you're at it?

"Maybe I'm not the guy you think I am," he says ominously.

So much for digging for compliments. I'm going to have to train him to recognize my methods a little better than that if this is going to work, obviously.

"I think I know you pretty well," I say with a confidence I don't really feel. His latest confession has me wondering. "I've known you since I was a kid."

"But you know the man you imagined me to be, not who I really am."

The knowledge that he might be right makes me profoundly sad. Did I fall in love with an ideal and not a real person? That would be a tragedy of epic proportions, to imagine that my entire life has been wasted pining away for someone who doesn't even exist.

"I hope not," I finally say, meaning those few simple words with all my heart.

"There's something else I have to tell you. Before you decide whether you want to have another date with me."

"What's that?" I take my drink and down most of it, burning my throat in the process. He was right. I think I need to be drunk for the rest of this. If the look on his face is any indication, his next confession will be even bigger than the first. I'm sipping the last bits of whiskey off my ice cubes when he finally answers my question.

"I have a son."

I choke on the ice cube that slides into my throat and end up doubled over, trying to breathe as he whacks me on the back.

Chapter Thirty-Two

A SON?" I FINALLY SAY when I have my breath back. I'm so happy I didn't vomit my chicken wrap on his coffee table; it was close for a few seconds there. "You have a son?" I can't compute this information. It just won't sink in. "Who? When? With whom? When? Who is he? How old is he? When? What's his name?"

Rob puts his hand on my arm gently. "Just relax. I'll give you all the details you want. Just don't... hate me until I'm done."

I pull away from him and squeeze myself as far into the corner of the couch as I can. "Fine." I'm glaring at him, but I can't help it. How can he possibly have a son without me knowing about it? Is he not like another brother to me? A *de facto* member of our family? Does he have a wife too? Holy shit, I need more whiskey.

I look around, trying to locate the bottle, but Rob is oblivious. He's staring at his clasped hands that rest between his knees as he sits forward on the edge of the couch. And so, his confession begins...

"When I was in law school, I had this girlfriend. Val." He glances at me. "Do you remember her?"

I shake my head numbly. Whenever I heard from James that Rob had a girlfriend — and now that I think about it, James was always especially happy to spread that news — I ignored the whole thing. I convinced myself that any girl he was with was a big mistake that he'd figure out eventually. And I'd be there waiting for him when he finally realized I was the girl for him, of course. Stupid, stupid me.

"We dated almost the entire three years we were there. Anyway, in our last year, she got pregnant."

"How?"

His smile isn't happy. "The way most people manage it. We used protection, but I guess it failed."

"Or she made it fail," I say bitterly. I know plenty of women like that, who see a great guy and think trapping him with a baby is a great way to tie him up for life. I hate to think that Rob fell for something like that.

He shrugs. "Doesn't matter. She had the baby, and I took responsibility."

"Except that no one in the world but her actually *knows* you have a son, so I'm not sure how that's taking responsibility." Rob has fallen a couple notches in my view. I never imagined him doing something like this, having a child and hiding him.

He sighs again, his shoulders sagging. "It's not that simple."

"So explain it to me," I say, sounding bitchy. "So I can understand. In real simple terms."

He looks up at me, his expression tortured. "Please don't say it like that."

I feel guilty and have to look away. "Whatever. Sorry."

"Don't apologize. I know you're angry. You should be. I'm angry at myself. I should have handled it differently. I should have handled everything differently. I've made a ton of mistakes, but the two biggest ones are how I dealt with the situation with Brian and how I handled it with you."

"Brian?"

He smiles sadly. "My son. That's his name."

I'm picturing a little toddler running around, but that can't be right. "How old is he?"

"He's thirteen."

"And how often do you see him?"

"Almost every weekend and some nights during the week."

I look around the room and see no evidence of a teenager here. There's not one single photo in sight. And I know for a fact that this place only has one bedroom.

"Does he stay over?" I ask.

"No. He can't."

I'm afraid what that says about Rob. Is he that cruel that he'd keep his teenage son from his life like that?

"Why not?" I'm trying not to cry. I really am. But I can't believe that the man I so admired has turned out to be so cold. My eyes are burning with tears I won't let fall.

"Because he's handicapped, and I don't have the facilities here to care for him."

A loud ringing starts in my ears and won't stop.

"What did you say?" I whisper. I'm sure I didn't hear that right.

"I said that he's handicapped. Severely. Taking him out of his home is very complicated and somewhat dangerous, so I visit him where he lives."

Tears overflow and start to slide down my cheeks. "What happened to him?"

Rob shrugs slightly. "Nothing happened, per se. He was born with cerebral palsy and there's no way to know how it happened. The doctors believe he was exposed to some virus or suffered some sort of brain damage during gestation. There's just no way to know for sure."

I reach out and put my hand on his arm. "I'm sorry." I'm apologizing for everything — for judging him, for the sadness I know he feels over his son, for whatever made him think he had to hide it from us. Are we that judgmental? Did he fear what we'd think if he told us the truth?

"Does James know?"

"Yes. He knows. He's the only one outside of our families who knows."

I'm hurt that James had that privilege before me, but I understand. Kind of.

"Whose idea was it to keep it a secret?" I can't imagine what a parent of a handicapped child goes through, but I want to believe I wouldn't be ashamed of my child. Is Rob ashamed or is it something else? Is Val?

"It was his mother's idea. I defer to her on everything. She's been through a lot."

"I can imagine." I scoot closer to Rob on the couch. "Is she okay? I mean, she must be, he's her son and she loves him, but... I mean..." The words won't come. I want to know everything about her and Brian too, but I don't want to push.

"She's fine. As fine as a mother can be seeing her child suffer."

"He's suffering?" The tears come more readily.

Rob turns his head to glance at me. "He's severely handicapped. He can't walk, he can't talk, he can't hear very well if at all. It's hard for us to know for sure if he can even process what he does hear. He's thirteen years old, but he only weighs sixty pounds. He gets bed sores very easily, every time he gets a chest cold we wonder if it will kill him." Rob shakes his head and rubs his hand through his hair distractedly. "It's not easy for either of us, but for her, it's worse. She blames herself."

"But why?"

"Because she's his mother. She carried him. That's all the excuse she needs. No one else blames her, of course, but every time she looks at him, that's what she's thinking."

"Your relationship never had a chance, did it?"

"Not after Brian was born. I tried. I really did. For his sake, more than anything. I cared about her, sure, but I never planned to marry her. But I would have once I knew she was pregnant, and I would have made it work. But she didn't want to."

"She turned you down?"

He smiles sadly. "She's a great mom. She told me she only had room for one man in her life after Brian was born, and he was that man. I got it. And I respected it."

"So what does she do? Does she visit him every day?"

"Pretty much. She reads to him, she gives him baths, she brushes his hair, she takes him in the therapy pool and walks around with him in there. She takes him on walks around the property." He shrugs. "She does whatever she can to be close to him."

"Where is he?"

"He's at a private facility outside the city. Harrington's it's called. There are only twenty patients there, so he gets great care."

"Will you take me there to meet him?" I hold my breath, waiting for his response. I'm nervous about it, but he's Rob's son. Of course I want to get to know him.

"If you really want to go," he says softly.

I rub his back. "I do. I want to meet your son. I'm kind of pissed I never knew about him before, actually."

Rob puts his glass down on the table and drops his face into his hands. It's only when I feel his back shaking under my hand that I realize he's crying.

I pull him against me and do the best I can to hug is broad back. "Shh, you don't have to cry. I'm not mad at you."

One of his hands comes away from his face and snakes around my waist. We sit there on the couch like that for a really long time, Rob sobbing into my lap and me crying above him. This is so not how I thought our first date would end up, but I'm not complaining. It feels like a whole new world has opened up in front of me and Rob is standing just beyond the door of it inviting me in. All I have to do is take the first step over the threshold.

Chapter Thirty-Three

I WAKE UP WITH A cramp in my neck from Rob's stupid couch. When I stretch my leg out it hits him in the face and he grunts. I crack an eye and see my big toe in his nose.

Yanking my foot back, I smile. "Oops. Sorry about that."

His eyes are only half open and his hair is everywhere. I've never seen Rob look so sexy. His shirt is almost completely undone, revealing the undershirt beneath. His pants are wrinkled and his belt is on the coffee table. It would be so easy to undress him right now...

"You want some coffee?" he asks, sitting up and scrubbing his head a few times.

A glance at my watch tells me we've only been sleeping about four hours, after staying up until the wee hours reminiscing about growing up in love and not knowing it.

"Not really," I say. I can't stop staring at him, he's so gorgeous. I'm completely lusting after him. His confessions and emotional breakdown last night only made him sexier. He's a father. A man who's suffered tragedy and survived. He respects the mother of his child and stands by her side as they do the best they can for their son.

So what if he made some mistakes? I've made plenty of my own, and I don't want anyone judging who I am now by the things I've done wrong in the past and regretted. It wouldn't be fair of me to do that to him. All my misgivings have disappeared. I know Rob. I've known him for most of my life. He's good and kind and loving and funny and sexy as hell. I'm so glad I slept over here, even though right now I know I look terrible, have stinky breath, and slept in the dress I wore last night on our first date.

He grins when he catches me staring at him. "What? Is it my hair?" He brushes at it with his hand, doing nothing to fix the mess that it has become.

"Yes. Among other things." I let my gaze slide over his body, starting with his gorgeous face and ending with his crotch.

His grin grows wider. "You'd better quit looking at me like that or we're both going to be in trouble."

"Oh yeah?" I lean in closer to him, hoping my breath isn't too horrible. "What kind of trouble?"

He stares at me intently as his hand comes up and settles behind my neck. "This kind," he says, pulling me toward him with a growl.

We come together like a car crash, bodies slamming into each other, things falling apart. I hear something breaking but ignore it. Maybe it's the coffee table, but who cares. A seam on my dress rips as he pulls it from my shoulders. The last three buttons on his shirt fly off as I give up on taking it off slowly.

He pushes me down the hall as we kiss, our tongues battling for position, hands everywhere. My back slams into his door, but a second later, I'm falling backwards as he opens it. He catches me and drags me over to the bed, the two of us stumbling and barely making it before we fall in a tumble onto the mattress. First he's on top, yanking my bra straps down and pushing my panties from my hips, then I push him over and bite his bottom lip before climbing on top of him.

I stare down at his wet lips, his crazy hair, his dark eyes and bare chest as I unhook my bra and throw it to the floor.

"You are so hot right now," he says, his hands sliding up to cover my breasts.

I grind my pelvis down onto his hard length, moving so I can feel it pressing into my panties that are still somehow in the way. My dress is gathered at my waist, also being very inconvenient. *Too many clothes, dammit.* Just as I'm trying to decide how to rid myself of all of it, Rob grabs me, flips me over onto my back, and yanks my panties and dress down to my ankles where they fall to the floor in a heap. *Whoo hoo, problem solved!*

He drops to his knees at the side of the bed and pulls me to him by my hips.

"What are you doing?" I ask breathlessly as his face lowers to my thighs.

"Just let me..." And then he's between my legs and I'm moaning.

There's no time for awkwardness or regret or wondering what he might be thinking. His tongue is driving me wild and soon I'm yelling for release. I've never been so turned on in my life.

He's gone for a moment and then he's back, this time looming over me with his entire body. "I need you now," he says, his face so dark he looks dangerous.

I reach down and find him naked, hard, and ready to go. Scooting back on the bed, I open my legs as my arms reach up to him. "I'm right here, waiting." And pulsing with need. I'm going to go insane if he doesn't get inside me like right now.

And then he's there, filling me, pushing into me so deeply I think I'm going to split apart. My hips strain upwards, bringing him even more fully into me.

We groan together, moaning, kissing and groping. My nails drag across his skin as the need builds inside me. He reaches down and grabs my rear end, squeezing and kneading as he thrusts into me. The pace of our rhythm increases and I find myself crying.

"Are you okay?" he asks, pausing.

"Don't stop!" I screech, grabbing him with both hands and lifting my hips as I beg for release.

He growls and surges forward, filling me and yelling out like a wild man. "Jana! Jesus! I'm coming!"

And then I fall from that cliff he led me to. I close my eyes and cling for life, hoping when I hit bottom I'll still be alive and he'll still want to be with me. I've never felt so fulfilled in my entire life as I do in his bed and in his arms.

Chapter Thirty-Four

I'M NERVOUS. I KNOW ROB and I have made it past our first hurdles — first date and sex, woo hoo! — But this trip is a much bigger deal than those things were. I'm about to meet Val and Brian, the two most important people in his life who I didn't even know existed until just two days ago.

"Are you nervous?" Rob asks, taking my clammy hand in his as we walk up the stately driveway of the home where Brian lives.

"Very. I think I'm going to barf."

"Barf?" Rob looks at me, kind of sad. That's when I realize he's misunderstood.

"No! Not barf like I'm grossed out. Barf because there are so many butterflies in my stomach." I hang onto his arm like I can't walk on my own. "I'm about to meet your first true love *and* your son. Anyone would be nervous in my shoes."

He detaches me from his arm so he can put it around me, holding me close. "Don't worry. Val knows you're coming and she's told Brian. They're expecting you. And she's happy for me."

"She is?"

"Of course. She knows how hard it is for me to be with someone."

I look up at him, curious. "Why is it hard for you? I don't understand." He's sexy, accomplished, single...

He opens the front door for me and waits for me to precede him before he responds. "You'll see."

People manning the reception area smile and nod at him.

"Hey, Rob," says a big guy wearing a white outfit and red sneakers, wheeling someone in a chair down the hall.

"Hey, Greg. What's new?" Rob reaches out to shake his hand.

"Same old, same old." The big guy's hand swallows Rob's smaller one. They both share a genuine smile with one another.

Rob turns to me and gestures. "This is Jana, my best friend's little sister."

My face turns pink as I shake Greg's hand.

"Uh-huh," Greg says, in a tone that reveals he's way more perceptive than he probably should be. He points to the person in the chair, a very frail girl with just a few wispy hairs floating around her head. "This is Rebecca. She's just going for her water therapy."

"Hi, Rebecca," I say, not sure what the protocol is. Should I shake her hand? Can she hear me?

She responds with a grunt and a wobbling of her head.

Greg pats her on the shoulder. "All right, all right, we're going." He talks in a loud whisper. "Water therapy is her favorite. She gets testy when I'm slow."

We watch as she's wheeled away and Greg starts talking to her about the weather outside. His voice fades out as they get farther down the hall.

"Are all the kids in wheelchairs here?" What I really want to know if they're all as bad off as she is. I can't imagine what that's like — to be locked inside a body that won't work but to have all the same thoughts and feelings I have in my able-bodied self. They must learn patience from a very early age.

"Pretty much. This is a skilled nursing facility, so everyone here needs help with all their ADLs."

"What's that?"

"Oh, sorry. I forgot you don't know the lingo yet. ADLs are actives of daily living, like eating, dressing, bathing, moving around, and using the bathroom. All the patients here need assistance with all of those things."

I want to say something, but the only thing that comes to mind is how sad it seems, and I know that focusing on the negatives is not the way to start this relationship with his son and son's mother.

"Here we go," Rob says, stopping outside a door covered in decorations.

"Did Brian do these?" I ask, touching one that shows two stick figures standing in flowers.

"With some help," Rob says, pushing the door in.

I wait outside as he walks in. The room has a hospital bed on one end, up high with several machines nearby. There's a round table with two chairs at it and a large wheelchair holding someone I can't see from behind, and on the other end of the room is an armoire, a sink, and a door I assume leads into a bathroom.

A woman sitting in the chair next to the wheelchair stands, smiling and smoothing down her pants.

"Rob, hi!" She looks down at her table companion. "Look, Brian, your dad's here."

Just hearing Rob being called a dad makes my heart clench up. I can't see his face anymore because his back is to me. I walk in a couple steps so they won't think I don't want to come in, even though I feel like I'm invading their private sanctuary.

"And daddy brought a friend with him," Val says, moving to welcome me. "Hi," she says, smiling warmly and holding out her hand. "It's so nice to finally meet you, Jana."

I take her hand and shake it, a little surprised to find out she's heard of me already. Did Rob tell her recently or has she known about me for a long time? When she said 'finally' it made me think he's mentioned me before yesterday. I feel a little warm glow starting over the idea.

Rob is bent down, talking softly to his son.

I look at Val, hoping she isn't sensing how nervous I am. "It's really nice to meet you too. Both of you." I let her hand go and look around the room. "This is a really nice place."

"It is," she says, smiling warmly, her brown eyes and beautiful Latina looks only slightly intimidating. "I agree. I couldn't ask for better, thanks to Rob." She looks over at her ex-boyfriend with admiration. "He works really hard so we can be here." With that, she turns and walks back over to the table, sitting down in her chair. Looking up at me, she gestures for me to join her in the other seat.

"Come on over and meet Brian," she says. She looks her son and smiles warmly. "He's been waiting to meet you all morning."

I walk over, my heart beating rapidly as I wonder what I'll see. I pray my expression won't reveal anything that hurts anyone's feelings. I've never known a handicapped child personally. I want to believe I'll do the right thing, but what is the right thing? I don't even know.

I come around the table and stop near Rob. He stands and moves back so I can get closer.

"Brian, this is my friend, Jana. She's James's little sister. Remember, I told you about her?"

I look down at the boy who's remained hidden from my world for thirteen years. His hair is dark like his mother's but his skin is lighter, more like Rob's. He's tiny, smaller than I imagined he'd be, with a very thin and angular face. His arms and legs are bent sharply at every joint in a way that looks very uncomfortable. His body is bent to the side, leaning toward his mother. He stares off into space, giving me the impression he doesn't even know I'm here. My heart goes out to him and his parents, and I have to battle to hold back the tears that want to burst out of me.

I bend down and touch his shoulder. "Hi, Brian. It's really nice to meet you." I have to look to the side and wipe tears away and clear my throat before I can continue. "What are you doing today? Drawing some pictures?" There's a paper on the table in front of him and a crayon.

"Yes, he is," says Val, taking her son's hand and the crayon together. She pulls his arm gently toward the table and uses her own hand to guide him with his drawing. "Today we're just doodling. Brian isn't in the mood to draw a picture."

Her hand jerks and then she smiles. "Or maybe he is in the mood. Let's see."

Rob's hand gently comes to my shoulder and rests there as we watch the crayon move. Val holds her hand steady, and I get the impression she's moving around the paper like it's a ouija board, letting her son's spirit create what's in his mind.

Slowly but surely, what looks distinctly like a happy face appears on the paper. Val lets the crayon drop and gently moves her son back into his chair. A shoulder harness seatbelt that she tightens holds him in place.

She looks up at me, her smile so bright it lights up the room. "Brian is happy to meet you too."

I stand, needing circulation back in my legs. Rob hugs me from behind, resting his head on my shoulder as he looks at his son. "He's a very talented artist," he says, his voice a little hoarse. "I have a whole book of his drawings at home."

A spark of inspiration hits me as I take a seat across from Brian at the table and take a paper and crayon for myself. "You should introduce him to Sarah," I say, drawing a house with a tree next to it.

Val sits back in her chair, resting her hand on her son's arm. "Who's Sarah?"

I smile, realizing that I'm now championing the woman who I blamed for helping to ruin my life. "She's my brother's wife. She's an artist. She works with paint, and she's really talented. Maybe she could come out and work with Brian a little some day."

I glance at Rob and he looks so hopeful and sad at the same time it makes me want to burst. I'm so going to sleep with him out in the parking lot.

"Did you hear that, Brian?" Val says, sounding very excited. "An artist! And you love painting, don't you?" She looks at me to explain. "He's worked with paint before, but it was always such a mess. We've mostly stuck with the crayons and colored pencils."

Brian starts jerking his head around and we all look at him.

"Okay, Buddy," Rob says, reaching out and stroking his son's face. "I'll bring Sarah out here to see you."

I swallow over and over to keep the tears at bay. I had no idea I could love someone this much. Whatever I felt before for Rob pales in comparison to what I'm feeling now.

Chapter Thirty-Five

AFTER AN HOUR OF COLORING and chatting, a few kisses and hugs shared with Brian and Val, we leave. His nap time has arrived and Val likes to have that time alone with her son. After having seen what she must go through every day, worrying about her baby, I can understand why Rob defers to her and does whatever he can to make her happy. Seeing him like this has made me realize I never really knew him at all, and he's way more amazing than I could have ever dreamed him to be.

"So where to now?" he asks, walking next to me down the long drive to the parking lot.

I lace my cold fingers through his warm ones and he stuffs them both into his coat pocket. "Wherever you want to go. Or do." I say, thinking about him naked. His apartment's over an hour from here. I'm pretty sure I'm not going to be able to keep my hands off him for that long.

He stops and I keep going. My hand in his pocket yanks me back. "What?" I ask, pretending like I don't know what's going on.

"Or do?" He grins. "Did I hear that right?"

I shrug. "Maybe."

He leans down, kissing me gently. Then he whispers against my mouth. "I know a really quaint B&B just down the street if you're interested."

I pull my hand from his pocket and grab the lapels of his coat, pulling him against me. "Oh, I'm interested, believe me."

He picks me up and grabs me, smashing his lips into mine. The kiss quickly grows hot as our tongues battle for position and re- mind us of other intimate invasions. "I can't get enough of you," he moans, his tongue sliding against mine, making me want to press my body into his more so I can feel every part of him.

"Me too," I say, breathless, needing to be out of these clothes immediately.

"Come on," he says, ending the kiss and hugging me fiercely before letting me go. "We need to hurry up or I'm going to do something I'll regret."

"Like having sex in the parking lot," I suggest as he drags me toward the car. I can totally picture it, the windows all steamed up, my feet on the windshield.

"Don't tempt me," he growls, looking back at me to scold me.

I wink. "Why not?"

The parking lot is surrounded by trees. Our car is not the only one out here, but there's no one around; everyone's either in the building, which we can't see from where we are, or they're out on the road, on their way to the parking lot. Or maybe there's no one on their way here. Maybe we'll be alone out here for a long time.

He walks me around to my side of the car and goes to open the door. I lean on it and stop him.

"What?" he asks.

"I need you now." I say, giving him that look that says I'm not kidding.

"The B&B's just..." He looks over his shoulder and starts to point, but I interrupt him by grabbing his coat and pulling him against me.

"Now." My hands go around his waist and I press my hips into his. He's already hard, and I know I'm ready.

He looks around desperately and then seconds later is undoing is belt. "You're completely crazy, you know that?"

I lift up my dress and slide my panties down, thankful that I thought to wear thigh-high stockings under my knee-high boots.

"Oh my god," he says in a rough whisper. "You're not wearing anything else under there?"

I lift my dress so he can see my stockings stopped at my upper thighs. "Nothing? I have stockings on." I say it with all innocence, but I know what it'll do to him.

His hard length drops out of the front of his pants and quickly finds my center. Rob grabs my leg and hikes it up to his hip, pressing himself into me as I get in better position. I'm so ready for him, he just slides right into me, filling me and giving me exactly what I wanted.

"Oh yes," I whisper, holding onto his shoulders. He slides out a little and then pushes in again. I meet his thrust, pushing my hips forward as far as I can. My legs tremble with the effort.

"Oh my god, I can't believe we're doing this," he says, dropping his head to my shoulder.

I can feel his entire body holding back his power as the muscles under his back and shoulders tense and release. We're both shaking with unspent passion and anticipation.

"Harder," I urge him. "I love it when you're in me like this."

His thrusts come faster and deeper. We've found our rhythm and every time we come together, he presses into my most sensitive spot and the heat builds. I'm rubbing on him, wanting more but unable to find it out here against the car.

He grabs my ass and uses it to pull me into him more. My back is digging into the car door, but I don't care. I need more.

All of a sudden, he pulls out. I glance around, worried we're about to be caught, but then he grabs me by the waist and spins me.

"Turn around," he demands. "Bend over."

My coat gets thrust to the side and my skirt flies up, baring my cheeks to the cold, but he's there a second later, sliding into me from behind, and I forget all about the winter weather. His hand comes around and his finger starts to massage me from the front as his hardness strokes me from the inside.

"Oh, Rob, my god…" I open my legs more and hold the door handle as he pushes into me from behind. My whole body bounces with every thrust and I start to moan with each one. I'm almost there. Almost…

"Oh, Rob. Yes, please. Oh my god…"

He leans over and whispers. "Shhhh, not too loud, baby, or I have to stop fucking you out here."

Just hearing him say that sends me right to the edge. "You are fucking me," I whisper back, almost like I'm crying. "Don't stop. Don't stop."

"You sure?" he asks. "You sure you don't want me to stop?"

I reach behind and grab whatever I can find, getting a fistful of his pants. I pull him to me and help him move faster. "Now. I need you now," I say, probably too loudly.

"I'm going to come," he says, his words given with effort.

"Me too!" I'm almost there. Jesus, it feels like I'm going to explode!

His finger slides along my sensitive spot as he starts to orgasm. His length gets bigger, thicker somehow and all of it combined is just exactly what I was hoping for, dreaming of when I saw him earlier. I knew it would be good, even out here in this stupid parking lot.

I gasp with the power of my orgasm and push against the car to steady myself as much as possible. He drops his hand and grabs my hips, slamming into me from behind. The two of us cry out in tandem and then, after almost a minute of tiny deaths, fall against the front of the car together. He slides out of me and breathes heavily in my ear.

"I can't believe we just did that," he says, sounding very tired.

"I can." I turn around, letting my skirt fall into place as he picks up his pants that have fallen to his ankles. Were it not for his coat, his bare ass would be hanging out for the entire world to see. Not that there's anyone out here to see anything, thank goodness.

He's buckling his belt when he looks up at me again, his gaze decidedly mischievous.

"What?" I ask, wondering what he has up his sleeve next.

"You still up for the B&B?"

"Hell yeah, I'm up for it."

He laughs and then pulls me into a hug. For a long time we just stand there holding each other. When he finally speaks, his words are more serious and muffled against my coat.

"I never knew it could be this way with you."

"What...? Sexy?" I laugh, maybe a little embarrassed that I let him do what he just did.

He pulls back and strokes my face as he stares at me. I see so much love in his eyes it's almost scary. "I always knew you were amazing and beautiful and funny and caring. Then when you took Cassie in, I knew what a great mom you were. And now, I know what an amazing, adventurous and fun lover you are. You're the whole package. Why did I wait so long to find out?"

I shrug, embarrassed by his compliments and maybe a little sad to think about Cassie. I'd done a good job of keeping her out of things until now. "I guess before it wasn't a good time."

"I listened to your brother when he warned me away over and over again. I'm not listening to him anymore."

"Are you sure?" I look up, all the vulnerability I have left in me showing in my expression. After so many years of hoping and dreaming and praying, it's hard to believe this can really be true.

"I'm sure." He leans down and kisses me, gently. Tenderly. Showing me in a way that words couldn't, how much I mean to him.

Chapter Thirty-Six

L YING IN BED ALL DAY with Rob is my dream come true. Better than my dream come true. Not only is the sex awesome, but the conversation is blowing my mind. To think... all these years I've been dreaming about him, and he's been dreaming about me too.

"I swear it's true," he says. "I used to invent reasons to come over to your house. I left stuff there so I could come back to get it later. I was always hoping you'd be alone and we'd be able to talk, but James always managed to be there. It was really annoying."

"James must have known what you were doing."

"Not at first. But then he found a picture of you I kept hidden in my wallet. Then it was all over."

"A picture of me? What picture?"

He grins and rolls over to reach the nightstand next to him. From his wallet he pulls a tattered and faded snapshot of the three of us in The Hamptons. I'm wearing that bathing suit he mentioned before with the tassels on the sides.

ELLE CASEY

"Oh my god," I say, taking it from him, so happy to find out that my obsession was mutual. "I can't believe it. You sly dog." I stretch up to reach his lips and give him a sexy kiss.

"Mmm," he says, when I pull back. "Better than I ever imagined."

I look at him suspiciously. "Tell me you didn't use this picture for dirty things."

He snatches it away from me and slides it back into his wallet. "I'll do no such thing."

"Hey!" I roll over on top of him and trap his hands on either side of his head. My breasts hang between us, but I have zero problems with self-consciousness with him. It may have something to do with the fact that we've had sex about five times in the space of twenty-four hours.

"Hey what?" He strains up, trying to kiss me, but I lean away.

"How old were you in that picture?" I ask.

"I don't know. Why?"

"I was eighteen. That means you were…"

He sighs. "Thirty."

"Thirty? You dirty old man."

He frowns, looking guilty, and I immediately feel bad. I lean down and kiss him, using extra tongue.

"I take it you like dirty old men?" he asks, smiling.

"I like this one." I let go of one of his hands and sliding my fingers down his ribs so I can feel the silky hardness I feel growing under me.

His hand on my wrist stops me.

"What? You don't want to?" I'm worried I've hurt his feelings calling him old. He's only thirty-eight. I think the age difference really suits us, too. Most guys my age act like children.

"Don't be ridiculous. Of course I want to."

"Then what's the problem?"

He tries to smile, but it comes out strained. "I, uh, kind of promised your family I'd come over for spaghetti dinner." He looks over at the clock on the bedside table. "If we leave in an hour, we can get there on time."

I climb off him and sit on the edge of the bed, gathering the sheets around me. "*We?*"

He moves to sit up behind me, resting his hand on my left shoulder while kissing my right. "Yes, we. I want you to go with me."

"I can't."

"Of course you can, don't be silly."

I grab a pillow and hug it. "It's not being silly to be hurt over things that happened."

"No, of course not. But at some point you have to move on. You have to do what's best for the people you love and suck it up."

I snort. "Since when did you become a therapist?"

"Since just now."

"Oh yeah? Well, don't quit your day job because you kind of suck at it."

He sighs and then nips my shoulder with his sharp teeth.

"Hey!" I twist away and glare at him. "What was that for?"

"For being sassy." He gives me a hard look. "Behave yourself or else."

I laugh a little, not sure I believe what I'm hearing. "Excuse me?"

"You heard me." He grabs me before I can respond and drags me over onto my side, right up over the top of him. He's spooning me from behind now, but is arm is clamped around me so I can't move.

"You'd better cut that out," I say, only half meaning it. My heartbeat is going like crazy and I'm getting wet between my legs at his angry alpha male tone. This is a side of Rob I've never seen before. The surprises just keep coming with him.

"Or what?" he says, his free hand coming around to slide into my folds. His hard length settles in behind me, pushing into me, letting me know he's about to take charge of the situation and I'm probably really going to like it.

I try to sound natural when I respond, but it's difficult. My hips are trembling with the effort of remaining still. "Or you're going to be sorry," I say at barely above a whisper.

He lifts my top leg and slides inside me from behind, pushing into me until I'm almost face down. He uses a hand around the front of me to stimulate me from that side while he slides in and out over and over. I arch my back to accommodate the movement, make it go deeper.

"I want you there with me," he says in a dark tone, right next to my ear.

"No," I say, pleading with him for release while at the same time denying his request.

He pushes me onto my stomach and grabs my hips, yanking them up high and exposing my backside to the cold air. His fingers stroke me softly, up and down as I arch my back to the max.

"Rob…" I plead. I need him inside me.

"You like that?" he asks, slipping a finger in.

"I need you."

"How about this?" he asks, slipping in a second finger.

"Please," I beg.

"Not enough for you, babe? You need more?" His thumb swirls around my nub, making me crazy. I swear, I'm pulsating with need at this point.

"Yes, dammit!" I finally submit.

"Say you'll come and I'll give it to you like you want it." His fingers leave me and his hands go to my hips. He's poised at my entrance, pushing just the tip of his length inside.

"I'll come, I promise! I'll come hard."

"Yeah you will," he says, burying himself in me inch by inch until I'm crying with passion.

He hangs onto my hips as he slams into me. With every jerking motion, with every time his body crashes into mine, I get closer. And then he's shouting and hammering into me over and over. I can't take it any more. I fall over the cliff like I've been pushed and I close my eyes, enjoying every second of the drop to the bottom.

Chapter Thirty-Seven

I'M GROUCHY THE ENTIRE WAY to Brooklyn from my apartment.

"I don't want to go." I say, getting more and more attached to the idea of running away, the closer we get to Jeremy's house.

Rob smiles, turning the wheel of his BMW with one hand, his other resting on the gearshift. "You said you'd come. I distinctly remember looking down at your gorgeous ass in the air and watching the words come out of your mouth."

I reach over and slap him on the chest, my face burning with embarrassment. "You tricked me. I meant *come* as in have an orgasm, not come with you to spaghetti dinner." Frowning, I stare out the front windshield. I really, really don't want to go. I'm not just putting on an act for him to sex me up and convince me otherwise. I'm not ready. I can't face them. I can't see Cassie yet. It's going to hurt too much. My heart is still broken.

"All's fair in love and war," he says.

"Why does this feel more like war than love?" I mumble.

He reaches over and takes my hand. "Hey, that's not fair. You know I'm doing this out of love, right?"

That word hurts. A sharp pain jabs me in the chest. "Love for whom?"

"For you of course. For your family."

Did he just say he loves me or was that just an expression? A slip of the tongue, maybe?

"Whatever." I don't care if he really loves me right now. All I can think about is seeing that sweet baby being held by Sarah or Jeremy and how much it's going to hurt. I won't be able to watch it. I'll run out of the house and turn it into a great, big, stinking mess. At least with me staying away no one has to deal with it head-on. Staying away seems like a really good idea. My fixer upper's just a few miles from here…

At the next traffic light, Rob pulls my hand over and kisses it, leaving his mouth there until I finally look at him. His eyebrows go up.

"What?" I finally say. I can't resist that look in his eyes and stay silent.

"Please just trust me. Everything's going to be okay. I promise."

I pull my hand away and stare out the window. I will not cry today. I won't. I can control my emotions, even if I can't control the fact that I'm in the car and headed somewhere I don't want to go.

We pull into my brother's driveway ten minutes later, and I remain in the passenger seat, refusing to get out.

Rob comes around and opens my door, taking me by the hand and pulling. "Come on now. Time to go inside. It's cold out here." He gives me a pained look when I just sit there. "Please?"

I sigh heavily but swing my legs out, using the helping hand he's offering to get up from the low-slung car. I won't look at him, though, and as soon as I'm on my feet, I let go of him.

He stops me as I try to walk by, putting a hand on my shoulder. "Hey."

"What?" I look up at him, my expression cold. He deserves this. He tricked me into coming and bet on my blossoming love for him being enough leverage to get me to here. It worked. I'm here, but I don't have to be happy about it.

"Would you try? For me?"

My mood makes me wicked. "Just because we're fucking now doesn't mean you can manipulate me into doing what you want me to do whenever you feel like it."

Now he has me in both hands and he's bending over to look me right in the eye. "Whoa, whoa, whoa … where is this coming from?"

I shrug my shoulders to get him off me. His hands fall away and he takes a small step back.

"Where do you think it's coming from, Rob? Did you really think you were just going to take me to a bed and breakfast, show me a good time, and then I'd just follow you along like a little puppy for the rest of my life?"

He steps back another pace and stares at me, his expression going pained. "Is that what you really think I did?"

Now I feel terrible, but I'm still angry and hurt enough to keep being a bitch. "Maybe. What else could it have been?"

"Oh, I suppose it couldn't have been the fact that I *love* you and want to be with you, could it? No, of course not. Never mind the fact that I've been dreaming about being with you for almost ten *years*!"

His face is red and he's yelling now. I want to stop him, but I can't. He's on a roll.

"You think this is all about you? That you're the only one with skin in this game? The only one with feelings on the matter? That you're the only one taking a risk? Well, think again, Jana! Think again!" His arms start waving and jerking around as he yells. "James has been my best friend for the better part of my life. He's been with me through thick and thin … through losing my parents, through Val and Brian, through you and Cassie. He's been there, and by being with *you*, I risk that friendship. He might never talk to me again after tonight. James… the guy who's been like a brother to me. But am I going to walk up those stairs and pretend like I just gave you a ride over here? Hell no. If you want to? Fine. I'll play along. But if it's up to me, I say fuck it. Let's just live our lives the way we want to and say screw you to whoever doesn't like it! If James decides to cut me off, oh well! I think you're worth it!"

ELLE CASEY

"Are you finished?" I ask in a small voice. My heart is breaking in two all over again, and this time it's not from pain. He said he loves me. He meant it. He's willing to risk everything just to be happy with me.

"Yeah! Pretty much!" He's still yelling, but his anger seems to be dissipating.

I walk over, loop my arm through his and start walking to the front door.

"What are you doing?" he asks, sounding tired.

"Facing the music. You ready?"

He stops and turns toward me, his expression anguished. "Are you sure? Now I feel bad that I pushed you into this. You're not ready, are you? We can wait. I'll cancel."

The door flies open and Leah is there, her face shining with happiness. "Hey, guys! You made it! Are you coming in?"

We look at her and then each other. I face her after I see the pleading look in Rob's eyes. "Yes, we're coming in."

"Awesome. Come see Cassie's new dress I got for her. You're going to die from all the cuteness." She holds the door open, oblivious to the stress that's already eating me alive.

Chapter Thirty-Eight

WE WALK INTO THE FRONT hall and relieve ourselves of our coats. I'm so temped to keep mine on, entertaining a short fantasy that I'm going to walk in and say hello and then leave. But no such luck. Cassie's there on the floor and Leah's fawning over her and waiting for us to *oooh* and *ahh* over the lacy dress she bought for her.

I have to admit. It is pretty darn cute. "Where did you get that?" I ask, bending down to see the detail on the front bib part. "The embroidery is amazing." Little bunnies are dancing with little chicks on a pink background.

"I know. She'd better not barf on it."

I stroke Cassis's soft cheek, pulling her attention away from her toy cell phone. She sees me and smiles. "Moo!" Her pudgy hands go out and she strains toward me.

My heart cramps, but I pick her up and hold her close, taking the cell phone toy away so I don't get bonked in the face with it. "Yes, your Auntie Moo is here. Did you miss me?" I whisper in her neck as hug her. "I missed you something terrible."

Rob comes up behind me and peers into the baby's face. "Hello there, Cassiopeia. Did you miss your Aunt Jana?" He tickles her and she wiggles to get away.

"I'm Auntie Moo, not Jana. Pay attention." I move around to help her avoid him.

Rob responds by playing peek-a-boo behind my back, sending Cassie into peals of laughter.

"I thought I heard grown-up voices in here," Sarah says, walking into the room.

I bounce Cassie, suddenly worried she'll want Sarah and not me. I have this insane need to be first in this baby's eyes and heart, even though I know it's not fair or good for her. Sarah's her mother now, not me. I need to let go, but it's so damn hard.

Sarah smiles at me, but keeps her distance. "You guys good in here? I just need to keep any eye on the sauce." She turns to leave, only hesitating long enough to get an affirmative nod from me before going.

Leah walks up and strokes Cassie's back. "That was for your benefit, you know. Leaving you in here with Cassie."

I close my eyes and let out a sigh. "I know."

"She doesn't mean you any harm."

"I know, Leah. I don't need you to tell me that."

Rob's voice intervenes. "Let's just give Jana some space tonight, okay?"

Leah holds up her hands. "I am. I will. I'm not pushing."

I look at my two friends and do my best to smile so they know I love them and I don't hold any bad feelings toward anyone. "I'm okay. I'm going to be fine. I just need a little time and some spaghetti or something."

Rob smiles at me warmly.

"Ew," Leah says, scrunching up her nose. "Is spaghetti code for sex or something? That's weird."

I start laughing so hard at the expression on her face I can't stop.

"What?" Rob is confused, which only makes it worse.

"I've heard of men calling their thingies weird names, but a spaghetti noodle? How can that possibly be a compliment?"

I have to put Cassie down on the rug. I'm afraid I'm going to drop her, I'm laughing so much.

"Did I miss the joke or what?" James asks, entering the room from the kitchen.

I clear my throat to answer, but Leah beats me to it. "You don't want to know, trust me."

Rob finally catches on and jumps in. "No, wait, you've got it wrong, Leah. That's not what she meant."

"Sure, babe. Don't worry, your secret's safe with me." She gives Rob an exaggerated wink.

James frowns. "What secret? Why do I feel like I showed up late to the party?"

Leah hugs him. "Babe, all in good time. Just be patient."

James looks from me to Rob and back to Leah. "Why do I feel so confused right now?"

Rob walks over and slings his arm over James's shoulders. "Because we are trying like hell to keep a big secret from you, and we're doing a terrible job of it."

James pulls away and looks at him funny. "What? What secret?"

I can't believe Rob's actually going to tell him right now. Shouldn't we get through the appetizers first, at least? But then as he starts to talk, I'm glad. Maybe James will pitch a fit and we'll be able to leave before I have to see Jeremy doing the daddy thing. Even thinking about it makes me hurt again.

"James, your sister and I have something to tell you." Rob puts his arm around my waist and pulls me near.

James shakes his head slowly, two red blotches showing up high on his cheeks. "No."

"Yes." Rob nods. "It's happening." He points to me and then him. "*This* is happening."

"No, it's not happening. I told you before…"

"Hey, Rob. Jana. When did you guys get here?" Jeremy walks into the room after pounding down the stairs. He stops when he gets next to his brother, and everyone but James looks at him.

"What's going on?" Jeremy asks, looking first at me, then at James. "What'd I miss?"

Leah walks up and stops in the middle of all of us. "Only the best gossip since I got knocked up!" She's grinning from ear to ear.

"Leah…" James is reaching for her, but she grabs his hand and rests it on her belly.

"Shush, Boo. Let me handle this."

"I don't think that's a good idea," he says, his mood still dark, but his hand on her belly definitely acting as a distraction.

"Sure it is. I'm the only one here with a cool head." She turns her attention to Jeremy as she flops her hand out toward Rob and me, like she has an invisible platter resting on it. "So, you see, Jana and Rob here, have finally decided to stop dinking around and playing games and get together."

"What?" Jeremy looks completely confused.

"Yes, you heard me right. They are together. A couple. How else can I say it?" She looks up at the ceiling and then smiles again. "Oh. I know. They are getting it on like donkey kong, know what I mean?"

"Okay, that's enough." James pulls her to him and wraps his hand around her neck as if he's going to hug her but then covers her mouth. "You shush now and let someone else talk."

She frowns at him but lets him continue to manhandle her. As I watch them, it's becoming clearer to me why these two are together. As odd a couple as they seem, it somehow works. Thank God, because his only other long-term affair was with Hilary and I would never want that chick as a sister-in-law.

It reminds me of Rob's confession, and I look from him to my brother. Does James know about Hilary going after his best friend? He'll never hear it from me. Their long-term friendship is already looking iffy over this affair with me.

"You two?" Jeremy asks, pointing at Rob and then me. "Since when?" He's smiling, thank goodness. I guess I don't have to worry about him.

"Since very recently." Rob turns a stern expression on James. "I know you told me to stay away, but I couldn't. Not after doing it for ten years."

Leah's mouth drops open and she yanks James's hand away. "Ten years? Damn. That's a long time to keep it in your pants."

"Leah, dammit!" James turns on her. "That's enough!"

She drops her head and looks up at him with a you-must-be-crazy expression on her face. "Seriously?" She's completely unfazed by his temper. I almost laugh at the spectacle, but get a grip on myself just in time.

James is ashamed now, I can read it all over his expression and his body language. "No, I'm sorry. I just ..." He runs his hands through his hair. "I can't deal with this right now." He leaves the room with long strides, disappearing into the dining room.

"I'll go talk to him," Leah stage-whispers, leaving the room as fast as she can waddle.

"I'll help," Rob says, following close behind, leaving me alone in the room with Jeremy.

Cassie crawls over and grabs onto my pant leg, using it to stand. She wobbles on her two feet, looking up at me. "Moo." She reaches one hand up, but the combination of all her new moves cause her to lose her balance and she falls onto her butt.

Jeremy looks at me as I lift Cassie up into my arms. "She misses you."

"Oh yeah?" I close my eyes as I sniff her precious head. "I miss her too."

"You don't have to stay away, you know. We want you here."

I shake my head, not trusting myself to speak. I'm going to cry, I know I am.

Jeremy continues. "I know it's hard for you. I know you hate me and Sarah."

I open my eyes, needing to fix this. "I don't hate you or Sarah. I wanted to, believe me."

Cassie reaches up and pats my cheeks. "Moo. Moo moo."

Tears rise up, much as I'm trying to will them away. "I just miss her too much, you know?"

Jeremy steps closer, rubbing his daughter's back. "Of course you do. You were her mom for nine months."

Cassie leans over for her father, basically doing a suicide dive to get there. I barely hang onto her bottom half as he grabs her and takes her into his arms. She opens her mouth and leans in, taking his entire nose between her teeth.

"Thank you for the kiss, Cassie. No biting this time."

I start to laugh when I suddenly recognize the small cuts on his chin. "Tell me she didn't eat your face." I point to his boo-boos.

"Oh yeah, she did. She's a monster."

Memories come flooding back. "Oh my god, she bit me on the shoulder so hard one day I cried."

"Try getting a chunk of your chin removed."

We both gaze at her, our eyes full of love. "I'm so sad that Laura missed out on all this," I say, a tear sneaking past my defenses. I wipe it away as quick as I can.

"Me too," Jeremy says, his voice suddenly rough. "But she's here. She's experiencing it from wherever she is." He looks at me, his eyes glowing with pain and happiness at the same time. "I really believe that."

I nod. "Me too. She was a force of nature. If anyone can visit from the spirit world, it'd be her."

Jeremy looks at the ground and then back at me. "Sarah and I would really love it if you'd come around more often. I swear. She mentions it more than I do. Please don't hate her."

I can't stand the sound of his voice and the look on his face. I grab him and Cassie in a hug. "I don't hate her. I don't hate anyone. I'm just really sad. I'm sorry I've been so mean."

"You haven't been mean," Jeremy says, hugging me back. "You're being human. I just hope you can forgive us and let us back into your life."

"Forgive you?" I pull away to look at him. "You didn't do anything wrong."

"Are you sure you really feel that way? You were pretty angry. At Robinson too."

I shake my head. "I'm over that. I wasn't being fair. I get it now. The most important thing is that Cassie's safe and happy, and I know she is. She's where she belongs."

A voice comes from the kitchen. "Soup's on!"

We turn toward the dining room, just as a loud crash comes from somewhere in that direction. Jeremy shoves the baby into my arms and runs from the living room with me right on his heels.

Chapter Thirty-Nine

I GET INTO THE DINING room just in time to see Leah bonking her boyfriend upside the head with a baguette. James has Rob in a headlock and they've already knocked over two chairs.

"Get off him, you animal! What's wrong with you?!" She beats him so many times, the bread breaks in half and crumbs go flying everywhere.

Sarah's standing in the doorway, holding a pot of sauce with her eyes bugging out of her head.

"What the hell are you doing?!" Jeremy roars.

The wrestling stops and both Rob and James look up at him.

"This is my home! What is your goddamn problem, James?!"

James slowly releases Rob's head and stands, straightening his shirt.

Rob stands and does the same, but then really quick punches James in the side.

James grunts, but does nothing in return.

"Somebody better start talking or I'm canceling this dinner." Jeremy puts his hands on his hips and stares at the men across the room.

"No one's canceling anything," Sarah says, walking in and putting the pot down on the table. "I've been cooking this sauce all day. It's home made."

"Start talking James. Or Rob." Jeremy glares at them one at a time. "No one touches that sauce until you tell me what's going on."

"I already told you what's going on," Leah says, rolling her eyes. "Geez. Weren't you listening?"

"Just because Rob and Jana are together does not explain why these two idiots think it's okay to break my dining room chairs." He walks over and holds one up, displaying its broken leg.

"I'm sorry about that," James said.

"Money talks, bullshit walks. Send me a check for six hundred bucks and we'll call it even." Jeremy turns to Rob. "Did you do something wrong?"

Rob shrugs. "Not from my point of view, I didn't."

"Mine either." I walk over and stand next to Rob, holding Cassie on my hip. "Sorry, James, but you can't stop this. We're together. We're going to see if this thing we've been thinking about for way too long is real. You just need to stay out of it."

"What's the big deal?" Jeremy asks James. "He's your best friend. He's like a brother but without the weird blood tie that would make this all very wrong." He kind of laughs at his own joke. "Seriously, I don't see what the big deal is."

"I do." Sarah sighs, looking at all of us. "If it doesn't work out, what happens then? James loses his best friend, and his relationship with his only sister becomes strained. I don't blame him for wanting to keep them apart. Not that I recommend that or anything, but I see where he's coming from."

I want to hate Sarah for what she said but I can't. How could I? She gets it. She understands my brother and she has compassion for him. And she's not judging us either. I think our family needs a referee like her around.

"Good, I'm glad we have that all worked out," Leah says, taking her seat. "Because I'm starving. Where are the noodles?"

Jeremy moves around his brother and goes into the kitchen. "Coming right up."

Rob looks at James and holds his hand out. "We good?" he asks.

James looks at Rob and then at me. I stick my chin out, daring him to defy me.

James shakes Rob's hand, gripping it hard enough that I see Rob wince. "Just don't hurt her, or I swear to God, I'll make that nose of yours twice as ugly as it is already."

We all laugh and move to our seats.

Leah sighs as she looks on the floor. "I guess there's no garlic bread tonight."

"Maybe next time use something else for your weapon," James says, kissing her on the head as he sits down next to her.

"How about next time you take your testosterone out into the backyard so I don't have to grab the nearest baguette."

"Done," he says, taking her hand in his and putting it in his lap.

Two seconds later he jumps and yelps and then glares at her.

I can't stop laughing for the next five minutes. Every time I look in their direction, all I can see is his surprised expression and Leah's sneaky smile.

"You happy?" Rob asks me quietly as everyone chats about what's new in their lives.

I nod. "Very."

"We okay?"

I nod again. "Very."

He leans in closer and whispers. "You want to get naked?"

I keep chewing, acting like he didn't just get me all revved up. "Very," I say when I think I can manage to not smile too hard.

Rob gets a goofy grin on his face and shoves a giant bite of food into his mouth.

"So what's new with you?" Leah asks Rob. "Other than the obvious?"

He puts down his fork as he chews and rests his hands on either side of his plate. Eventually, everyone realizes that he's about to say something interesting, so the rest of the conversation dies off and we listen to what he's going to say. I'm very nervous he's about to make some kind of declaration about our love, which would be awesome on one hand, but terribly embarrassing on the

ELLE CASEY

other. This relationship is so new; I don't want to jinx it by calling it something big too prematurely, even though I know in my heart that Rob is the man for me.

"I actually have some very big news that's been about thirteen years coming."

The number thirteen strikes me as important, but I don't realize how important until he starts to elaborate.

"Fourteen years ago, when I was finishing up law school, my girlfriend Val became pregnant."

You could hear a pin drop in the room. Even Cassie seems to understand what's expected of her. She plays quietly with her noodle pieces, pushing them around her high chair tray with her finger, trying to get one to stick.

"She gave birth to my son, Brian."

"You have a son?" Jeremy asks. He looks over at James. "Did you know about this?"

James nods, his face a mask.

Leah bumps him on the arm. "Hey! You didn't tell me about Brian!"

"Just listen," he says softly, staring at his best friend.

"Brian was born with severe cerebral palsy. He's lived in a skilled nursing facility his entire life."

"Oh my god," Sarah says. "Where?"

"About an hour and a half from here."

I know what the unasked questions are, so I elaborate, worried they'll think less of Rob if they don't know the whole story.

"He needs expert nursing care around the clock. And it's a really, really nice place. His mom is there a lot and so is Rob." I look up at my man with shining eyes. I love him so much I can't even say how much.

"How long have you known about Brian?" Jeremy asks me.

"I just met him the other day."

"Babe, this isn't about you," Sarah says, nudging him.

"No, of course not." Jeremy shakes his head. "I'm just surprised is all. How come you didn't say anything?"

His insinuation is clear. Are we judgmental people? Was Rob worried what we'd think or say behind his back?

Rob shrugs. "It was what his mother wanted. She was worried that having a bunch of people come in and out of his life would be difficult for him. That he could get attached to someone who'd get busy and not come around anymore, and we're never sure how much he understands when we try to explain things."

"Oh." Jeremy looks down at the table and then at his own daughter. "I get it."

"Sarah," I say, the offer I made on her behalf jumping into my head, "I was wondering if you've ever done any work with hand-icapped people. With your painting, I mean."

She smiles. "As a matter of fact, yes. When I was in college, I did an internship at a center for adults with disabilities."

"Brian likes to draw with his mom," I explain. "They use crayons and pencils, but I suggested that maybe you'd like to help him paint."

"She doesn't have to do that," Rob says, hurrying to cut off Sarah's reply. "It's a long drive, and with winter, that makes it really hard to get there. Plus she's busy with Cassie."

"No, I'd love to." Sarah's face is glowing. "Seriously. If Jana doesn't mind helping me with Cassie, I could do it. Maybe once a week? Once every two weeks? Whatever you and his mother think is a good idea." She looks at Jeremy. "I told you something would come up."

Jeremy looks out at us and shrugs. "I've been trying to get her out of the house, and she's been telling me she'd go when she was ready." He looks at her and smiles warmly. "Taking care of Cassie is a job and a half."

It doesn't hurt quite as much to hear Jeremy say that as I know it would have yesterday or even an hour ago. Rob squeezes my hand under the table and I know he understands.

"If you want to come, that'd be great," Rob says. "Even if it's just once. Val and I talked about it, and we decided that Brian's old enough now to have some more transient type relationships. We're not worried as much about explaining why people are there or not." He looks around the table. "Change is good, right?"

"A necessary part of living," Leah says. "Now can someone please pass me the salt?"

"No." James says, glaring at everyone. "No salt for you."

She pouts at him and grumbles as she gets her next bite of noodles on the fork. "Party pooper."

When I laugh, I feel like I'm filling with helium, I'm so light. I'm not even really sitting on my seat anymore. I never would have imagined this night going this well when Rob first suggested I come. I'm so glad I listened to him. I'm so happy I have him in my life now, and not as my brother's best friend who I'm crushing on from afar, but as my boyfriend. And maybe in the not too distant future, something even more.

"We good?" Rob asks me as we dig into our dessert.

"Yes," I say, watching Cassie feed her daddy a handful of cake. She smears it all over his face, but all he does is try to lick it off, leaving her to do her worst, which she happily continues to do. Sarah watches them off to the side, smiling with her gaze full of love. "Better than good."

Chapter Forty

I'M STANDING IN THE MIDDLE of my fixer-upper that's now almost completely done. My hardwood floors are glistening with the new wax coating they just got, and the stain my contractor used matches the beautiful muted gray/green color I put on the walls perfectly.

Rob stands next to me, wiping his hands off on a rag. "Not bad at all," he says, looking around and nodding in admiration.

"More like excellent."

He comes over and kisses me softly on the lips. "I never had any doubts."

The doorbell rings, and I leave my lover to go answer it. I have one more walk-through to finish up before I call it a day over here and go back to Rob's place where I've pretty much moved in. Three months ago we both decided that the commuting between my place and his was getting annoying. And now we've made plans to move in here together, two miles away from my brother and his wife and Cassie. I couldn't be happier.

I open the door and smile at who's standing there on my porch. "Jake! I'm so glad to see you!" My tall plumber acts like he's going to shake my hand, but I take him into a hug instead. He quickly changes stride and hugs me back.

"Nice to see you too." He stands back straight, looking around the house from the foyer. "Wow. You've gotten a lot done since the last time I was here."

"I know, right? Come check it out."

Jake and I proceed into the living room, and Rob steps over to shake his hand.

"Hey, how's it going?" Rob asks.

"Well. And you?"

"Couldn't be better." Rob hangs his arm over my shoulder and smiles.

I recognize Rob's peeing-on-the-territory thing for what it is and stay there. I don't need him getting jealous over feelings I don't have for the plumber.

"Did you get that faucet changed out?" Jake asks. "If not, I have one in the truck."

"I fixed that," Rob says. "No problem at all."

"Great. And the gasket around the sink drain?"

"Fixed that too," my boyfriend volunteers, sounding very proud of himself. He might as well whip his pants down and start comparing penis size. I roll my eyes.

"Awesome. I guess you've been kind of doing my job for me around here." Jake looks at me. "Sorry about that. Big job over in Long Island was killing me."

"No problem," I say, poking my thumb at my boyfriend. "I have Mister Fixit here taking care of things." And not just things with my house, but my heart too. He's fixed everything.

Jake nods, looking Rob up and down before turning his attention back to me. "Good for you. Really. I'm happy for you."

I walk out from under Rob's arm toward the hallway. "Come check out the window seat he made me. You're going to love it."

Jake follows me into the master bedroom where Rob not only built me a cushioned window seat with storage underneath, but a whole wall full of custom book shelves. Crown molding rings the ceilings and baseboards six inches tall frame the floors. It's my dream bedroom.

Jake's gaze moves around the room, and he walks over to run his fingers on the fine wood of the shelves. "He does good work. Is he a contractor?"

I laugh. "No, he's a lawyer if you can believe that."

"Huh." Jake looks at the window seat and then at me. "You seem really happy."

"I am." I grin. "Come see what he did in the other room."

Jake follows me into the guest room where we installed a huge window that looks out into the back yard. A box of freshly plant-ed spring flowers are just outside, the tops of their many colored petals peeking up above the windowsill.

"Nice." He takes in the crown molding, the huge closet, and the attached bathroom.

"It's handicap accessible," he says, standing in the entrance.

"Yeah." I lean on the doorframe. "Rob's son has cerebral palsy. We've been talking about having him over for a sleepover once in a while."

Jake turns to look at me. "Where is he? With his mother?"

"At a skilled nursing facility." I point to the two beds, one regu-lar twin-sized and one hospital bed with side rails. "Hence the second bed for the nurse."

Jake turns and stands in front of me, looking down. "You changed your life."

I shrug. "A wise friend once told me I just needed to start look-ing at things differently and then my life could be different."

"Sound kind of far-fetched," he says, the hint of a grin there.

"Yeah, it's a little new agey for me, but what can I say; the proof is in the pudding."

He looks around. "The proof is in the changes you made. Good for you." He envelopes me in a strong hug. "I'm really happy for you."

"Thanks." I pull away and smile. "So maybe you can bring your dog by sometime when Brian is here and we can all watch him perform."

Jake looks out to the backyard. "There's not much room out there, but if you guys want to meet us at the park, we'd love to show off for ya. We've been working all winter, and Bosco's ready to run off all this extra energy he's got."

"Cool." I gesture for him to follow me as I walk out into the living room. I stop under the new chandelier that used to be a hole where mice fell out on innocent people's heads, and I shake Jake's hand. "It's a deal. The next really sunny day and we're there."

"Great. So, is there anything you need me to do?" Jake asks. "Plumbing good?"

"It's all good." I pull out a pre-filled and signed check from my back pocket and hand it to him, the last payment for all his work. "I'll be in touch for my next project. And for the performance."

"Performance?" Rob walks up, drying his hands off on a towel.

"Jake has a frisbee-playing dog, and I told him maybe when Brian comes for a visit, we could all go to the park and watch."

Rob's smile is slow in coming, but it's real. "That might be cool. I'll run it by Val."

I nod at Jake. "Val will love it. Trust me. And you'll love her. She's awesome."

Rob jabs me with his elbow, but I ignore him.

"Talk to you soon?" I say to Jake as I walk him to the front door.

"Absolutely. Just text me when you want to go to the park."

"Will do." When I shut the door behind him, I turn to glare at Rob. "What's up with the elbow to the ribs?"

He shrugs, grinding away at his fingers with the towel. He has a permanent layer of glue on his hands that he says makes his clients suspicious. "Nothing. Just didn't want you to encourage him too much."

Rob's tone is funny.

My eyes narrow as I try to figure out what he's thinking; I sense jealousy, or concern, maybe. "Encourage him? About what? Or whom? Brian or Val?"

Rob turns to go into the kitchen. "Neither. Whatever. Are we ordering pizza for dinner or what?"

I catch up to my silly boyfriend before he can escape into the dining room. "Hey," I say, making him turn around and hug me, "you don't need to worry about Jake. He's a good guy, I promise."

"Oh yeah? How do you know? Val's very special to me, you know. I don't want you hooking her up with just any guy."

I lean back and frown at him. "Does that sound like something I'd do?"

He sighs. "No."

"Okay, then stop it. Just hug me."

He throws his towel on the counter and bends over a little, enveloping me in his strong arms.

"Thanks for fixing all the things around the house," I say into his shoulder.

"You're welcome."

"Thanks for fixing me."

He kisses my neck. "You weren't broken."

I kiss his neck, pulling his shirt out of the way so I can reach his sensitive skin. "My heart was, but it's not anymore."

"I love you, you know." He pulls me in even tighter, almost taking my breath away.

"I love you too, babe." I lean my head back. "You okay?"

He nods, his eyes shining as he looks down at me. "I just can't believe you're mine."

I smile. "Yours? Well, I'm not sure I'd go *that* far. I am an independent woman, you know."

He digs around in his pocket and holds something up that he pulls out of it. "Oh, then I guess you wouldn't be interested in something like this, then."

I back up really fast, focusing on his hand. "Something like what?"

He shrugs, acting like he's going to put the jewelry box back into his pocket. "Oh, nothing."

"Nothing, my butt." I jump toward him, reaching for his pants.

He holds the velvet box high above his head. "Easy now. Don't get grabby."

I calm down immediately and stare at him, giving him my evil-eye. "Give me that box."

He laughs. "And here I thought I was going to have to convince you to say yes."

"Say yes to what?" My heart feels like it's burning a hole in my chest. If that box has earrings in it, I'm going to use the nail gun on him, I swear to God.

He lowers the box until it's between us and slowly pries the top off. "Say yes to my proposal."

I stare at the glittering monstrosity of a ring buried in black velvet.

"What proposal?" I whisper, mesmerized by my life, by what's happening in it, by the craziness that's obviously taken over my reality.

When he lowers himself down onto one knee, my hands fly to my mouth. It's not so much a reaction of shock as it is the fact that I'm afraid I'm going to vomit on him. This can't possibly be happening, can it? I've dreamed of this moment since I was so little I was still wearing princess costumes on halloween. He was my dream prom date, even though he was a grown man not interested in high school dances. His was the face I saw whenever I pictured my Prince Charming.

"Jana Oliver ... would you do me the honor of becoming my wife?"

I start to cry, and those cries quickly turn to sobs.

He frowns, his face falling. "Please tell me that's a yes."

I drop to my knees in front of him and grab him into a hug. Or maybe I'm just trying not to drown in the emotions, and he's my life raft, keeping me afloat.

Amidst my loud and sloppy blubbering, I manage to finally answer. "Yes! Yes! Of course it's a yes, you idiot! I've been waiting for this my whole damn life!"

He laughs, holding me close. "You have the strangest way of expressing yourself sometimes."

I pull away and hold out a trembling hand. "Just put that thing on me before I change my mind." As if that would ever happen. Ha!

He grabs the ring out, throws the box over his shoulder, and shoves the ring onto my finger. Then he sits back on his heels and wipes his hand over his forehead. "Phew! That was close. Almost lost you there."

I tackle his gorgeous self to the kitchen floor and quickly go about showing him just how *not* lost I am to him.

Chapter Forty-One

I HAVE TO HAND IT to Leah; she sure knows how to put together a wedding. And the fact that she did it with a newborn in her arms the entire time is pretty damn impressive.

I'm looking out Brian's bedroom window the white folding chairs on the lawn, arranged to face the arbor erected just this morning for the big event. Our family and a few close friends are milling around, waiting for the announcement that I'm ready. My cell phone rings, and I look down at the number on the screen. Smiling, I press the green button and put it to my ear.

"Hello, Rose. So nice to hear from you." I can't stop smiling. Today is the perfect day.

"Hello, Jana. I didn't want to bother you; I was just calling to say congratulations. I wish I could be there with you."

"You are in spirit," I say, looking at the amazing flower arrangements adorning the arbor in my yard. "The flowers are gorgeous. It's like Spring all over again in my backyard."

"Oh, wonderful. Please tell Robinson I send him my love, would you?"

I smile at how well she and Rob get along. They've spent countless hours discussing Rose's past and her career as an archeologist, something he studied in college but never pursued. It makes me just the tiniest bit sad we'll be living here and not across the hall from her. "I will, I promise."

"And don't be a stranger. My door is always open and my teapot always ready to be warmed up with some nice Earl Grey."

"I'll be there Sunday, after my honeymoon. You're going to give me a knitting lesson, remember?"

"Oh yes! Of course. I'm looking forward to it."

"Me too. Bye, Rose, and thanks again."

"It was my pleasure. 'Bye, Dear."

My heart feels like it's going to burst with love coming at me from all sides. I can't believe this is really happening to me.

The bedroom door opens and closes behind me, distracting me from counting my blessings, and I turn to look at my visitor.

"Hey, Val," I say, smiling at her. I look back out the window and see Brian in his wheelchair, a nurse standing nearby to keep an eye on him. He's wearing a tux specially made for his big day as Rob's best man.

"Hey there. Nervous?" She stops next to me, looking out the window at the pretty scene in front of us.

"Not really. Just standing here thinking about how lucky I am."

"You are lucky. Blessed. And Rob's lucky to have you in his life. We all are."

I hug her, my eyes tearing up. "Thank you so much. You have no idea how much it means to hear you say that."

She clears her throat as she pulls out of the hug. "I have something for you." She pulls something out of her purse and hands it to me. "I wasn't sure if you had something borrowed or blue, so I brought you this."

I take the lovely hair comb from her hand and smile. "I didn't. Thank you so much."

She walks over to the mirror above the dresser. "Come on, I'll help you put it in."

My hair is already up, and the comb with sapphires and diamonds matches my necklace perfectly as it slides into place

"Gorgeous," she says.

"It's perfect." I kiss her on the cheek. "Thank you for loaning it to me. I'll take good care of it."

She waves her hand. "Keep it. It's my wedding gift to you. Rob gave it to me several years ago, but I've never worn it."

"Are you sure?" I feel bad taking a gift from the father of her son. Is it wrong to love it so much anyway?

"Absolutely. I'm not much for bejeweled hair combs. I don't go anywhere but to see Brian and the grocery store." She gestures out to the yard. "This is as fancy as it gets for me, and I'm not much for standing out with shiny things."

I turn around and catch Jake standing off in the corner, looking at a sprinkler head. I bite my lip, wondering if I should get involved.

"How would you feel about a date in the park? All of us. To watch a dog play frisbee."

She shrugs, oblivious to my machinations. "Sure. I guess. Sounds like fun."

"With Brian of course."

She brightens. "Yes, that would be nice. I think he'd like that."

"Awesome." I put my hand on her shoulder and point to Jake. "See that guy out there?"

"The tall one?"

I grin at her. "Yes, and you can go ahead and say what you're really thinking. The tall devastatingly hot guy in the blue shirt."

She grins and looks at the floor, her face going pink. "Okay."

"Anyway, he has this amazing dog who can catch frisbees, and he's invited all of us out to watch."

"Not all of us," she says, sounding embarrassed.

"Yes, all of us. I told him about you and Brian, and he said you should come along."

She shrugs. "I don't know. Maybe."

"Come on," I say, taking her by the hand, acting like she's not giving me the blow off. "I need to get married." I'm not going to give her time to say no to me. I'll just let her marinate in the idea of watching this guy in action while I tie the knot with Mister Fixit. She'll come around eventually. How could she not? Jake's amazing.

Leah sees me through the back door, coming closer with Val by my side, and shouts loud enough for the entire block to hear her.

"Here she comes, everyone! Get in your seats! Come on, chop, chop!"

Everyone scrambles to follow her orders as she walks over and turns on a portable CD player. The wedding march comes out over the speakers set up in the tiny yard.

Jeremy and James assemble themselves near the end of the narrow aisle, each one holding his child in his arms. Brian is next to his father, who waits for me just in front of the arbor. Sarah and Leah are at the back door, grinning hugely.

Val breaks away and goes through the door. "Good luck," she whispers as she goes down the stairs and finds a chair at the front, near her son.

I pause at the back door and smile at my man — the guy who was the star of every dream I've had for the past almost twenty years. The ring on my finger, the cream-colored lace dress, and the bouquet in my hand say I'm getting married today, but I almost can't believe it's true. It's too good to be true. Is this just a dream? If it is, it's a hell of a cruel one. To get this close and find out it's all make-believe? No way. I'd never make it. Too much of my heart and soul are wrapped up in this affair.

Rob breaks away from his best men and comes striding down the aisle toward me.

"What are you doing?" Leah demands. "That's not how this is supposed to work."

Rob grabs the door, pulls it open, and fixes me in a powerful stare.

"What are you doing?" I ask, grinning from ear to ear.

"I can't wait anymore." He points behind him. "Get your butt down that aisle before I lose my mind."

I close my eyes, hold my arms out, and fall forward. The cool summer breeze whistles past my ears just before he catches me in his arms and holds me close, squeezing me so hard I lose my breath for a moment.

"I love you, Jana Oliver," he says in my ear, inhaling deeply and then kissing my neck.

"I love you too, Rob. Thank you so much." My eyes remain closed as he slowly turns me around and sets me on my feet in the grass.

When I'm on the ground again, I open my eyes.

Rob is staring down at me. "What are you thanking me for?"

I have to swallow my emotions down before I can speak, worried the happy tears will drown my voice out before I can say what I have to say.

"I'm thanking you for fixing things. For fixing things with Jeremy and Sarah and Cassie. With James. With me. With us."

He leans down and kisses me very gently on the lips before backing away. "It's me who should be thanking you for being so damn patient with me. It took me way too long to do this." He glances at the aisle.

"Better late than never."

He grabs both my hands and kisses the back of them. "Hurry up. I'll be waiting for you." And then he jogs back up the aisle and stops when he reaches his brothers from another mother.

I link my arms with Leah's and Sarah's and take my first step toward the rest of my life. As I reach the edge of the white runner, I swear I can see the vague outline of a girl who looks just like Laura standing in the place where my maid of honor would be.

What to read next …

For more of the humor, romance, and writing style you enjoyed in Love in New York, try JUST ONE NIGHT, my 6-part serial romance , available at all major online book retailers or through your local bookstore.

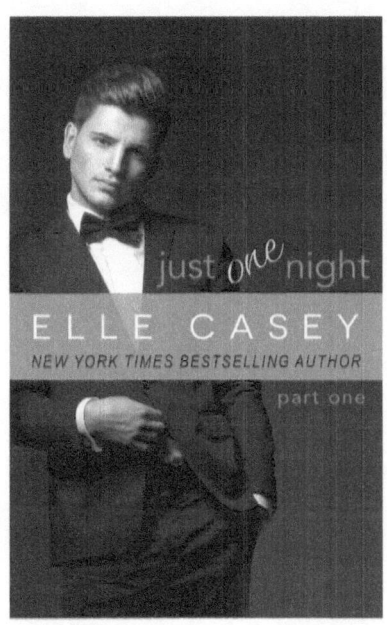

Being an independent author, I depend entirely on *you*, the reader, to get the word out about my books. If you liked this book, won't you please leave a review online and recommend it to a friend? The more you spread the word, the more books I can write, and nothing would please me more than to put a new book in your hands every single month.

I read all my reviews!

Find more Elle Casey books at the following retailers:

Amazon
iBooks
Barnes & Noble
Google Play
Kobo
Walmart
Your Local Library via the OverDrive ebook platform

ABOUT THE AUTHOR

Elle Casey, a former attorney and teacher, is a NEW YORK TIMES, USA TODAY, *and Amazon bestselling American author who lives in France with her husband, three kids, and a number of horses, dogs, and cats. She has written more than 40 novels in less than 5 years and likes to say she offers fiction in several flavors. These flavors include romance, science fiction, urban fantasy, action adventure, suspense, and paranormal.*

A personal note from Elle …

If you enjoyed this book, please take a moment to leave a review on the site where you bought this book, Goodreads, or any book blogs you participate in, and tell your friends! I love interacting with my readers, so if you feel like shooting the breeze or talking about books or your family or pets, please visit me. You can find me at …

Other Books by Elle Casey

CONTEMPORARY URBAN FANTASY

War of the Fae (10-book series)
Ten Things You Should Know About Dragons
(short story, The Dragon Chronicles)
My Vampire Summer
Aces High

DYSTOPIAN

Apocalypsis (4-book series)

SCIENCE FICTION

Drifters' Alliance (ongoing series)
Winner Takes All (short story prequel to Drifters' Alliance,
Dark Beyond the Stars Anthology)
The Ivory Tower (short story standalone, Beyond the Stars: A
Planet Too Far Anthology)

ROMANCE

By Degrees
Rebel Wheels (3-book series)
Just One Night (romantic serial)
Just One Week
Love in New York (3-book series)
Shine Not Burn (2-book series)
Bourbon Street Boys (4-book series)
Desperate Measures
Mismatched

ROMANTIC SUSPENSE

*All the Glory: How Jason Bradley Went from
Hero to Zero in Ten Seconds Flat*
Don't Make Me Beautiful
Wrecked (2-book series)

PARANORMAL

Duality (2-book series)
Monkey Business (short story)
Dreampath (short story standalone, The
Telepath Chronicles)
Pocket Full of Sunshine (short story & screenplay)

www.ingramcontent.com/pod-product-compliance
Lightning Source LLC
Chambersburg PA
CBHW020100180626
46812CB00006B/2414